Oli's Uncommon Cents

By Deborah Allen

Oli's Uncommon Cents
by Deborah Allen
Illustrated by Sophie Mattinson

Printed in the United States of America

ISBN 9781619966109

www.xulonpress.com

*Dedicated to little Grandma, and all young souls
who love adventure, believe for the impossible, value
the simple life, and treasure a dollar forty-one.*

Acknowledgments

Thank you, Susan Hodgin, for your expert editing and creative critiques. When in life we find a selfless person, who, without motive, invests and believes in our dreams, we have found a great treasure.

Thank you, Sophie, for sharing your amazing talents and gifts with me, Oli, and our Cents.

Thank you, Jim, for allowing me to grab at the stars and live out my dreams.

Chapter 1

The Nightmare

*I*f it was the tapping at the door or my nightmare, I'm not sure, but I shot out of bed like a launched rocket. Looking down at my red polka-dotted pajamas, I wondered why the dots were not bouncing in rhythm with my pounding heart. Every pore of my skin dripped with sweat, making my pajamas stick to me like a second layer of skin. The tapping persisted at my bedroom door. Staring around the room, I tried to separate nightmare from reality. The best I could do was set both feet on the cold tile floor.

It was nearly the same dream that I'd had every night for the last two weeks, but now I realized that they were only the dress rehearsals for last night's granddaddy nightmare. It began the same: Me and Geepa walking down a straight gravel road with dust from the farm fields swirling around us, not touching us. He was humming a song that I'd heard before, and the heels of his shoes were firmly crunching on the gravel. We were laughing and holding hands as we walked, but this is where the dream changed to nightmare: the road disappeared, dropping off into complete darkness. I could see only a small hill, then nothing. As we neared the hill, Geepa let go of my hand, and I was left holding his coin pouch. I looked down, and when I looked up, he was gone. I was left standing alone in a dark void, hearing only the sound of something tapping. I was terrified.

The tapping stopped, but I heard Mama's quiet voice say, "Oli, open your door." I couldn't speak. I sat at the edge of my bed staring at my feet. My thoughts swirled like the dust in my dream. I tried to review facts.

Reality slowly returned. Geepa was dead. Life at this point, dream or not, was a nightmare. The horrible sick feeling that I was going to cry boiled up inside me, but I was too tired to fight it.

This crying had to stop. My eyes were swollen shut, but I was at least able to see that my feet were still planted on the floor. The morning breeze from the open window blew through my room, making me shiver. Happiness was something that I could barely remember.

"Laugh," I said quietly to myself between my sobs. "How, and what's to laugh at?"

I looked around my huge room and found nothing funny. My worn out jeans and t-shirts were the only thing even slightly funny. I quietly snorted in humorous disgust, thinking of what Dad would say about the way I dressed. "In case you forgot, Oli, we have lots of money; you don't have to dress like some kind of vagrant tom-boy." Yeah, whatever. I didn't care about his stinkin' money or what he thought of me.

Looking away from my dirty pile of clothes, I

saw stuff, dumb meaningless stuff. "Why do I need all these stupid girly things?" I whispered to myself. Why did anger always come after sadness? I forgot all about laughter, which for a twelve-year-old was really pathetic. Kids my age were supposed to laugh and to be happy.

For as long as I can remember, I'd been given everything a girl could need, but that didn't make me happy. What I really needed was a backpack big enough to hold a week's worth of food, bus fare to Cardboard City, and hiking boots sturdy enough to hike through Idaho's Clearwater mountains. Fat chance, I'd get any of those things.

When we moved to northern Idaho seven years ago, Dad insisted on buying a huge, expensive house on the tallest hill in town. I was embarrassed to live in it. *He* didn't have to put up with all the teasing from school girls. "Who's your daddy, Swanky," they'd tease. What are the chances my last name would be Swank, something else I wish I could change about my life. Dad would say that it was embarrassing for a girl to dress and act like I did, but I didn't care how I looked; I didn't care that boys were my only friends. Maybe someday he and Mama would have another kid, maybe another girl, and he would get his chance to have the little paper doll girl who made him proud.

Lying back in bed, I stretched my arms and fluffed the pillow under my head. This was my life, like it or not. As I rested against the soft, down pillow, my mind wandered back to laughing. I let the good thoughts of Geepa replace the swirling in my head, thinking of the last Saturday I had spent with him.

Then something caught my eye, and the dream came back to me. It shimmered and caught the light coming through the window, sending bright flashes all over my room. It was the metal clasp on Geepa's coin pouch. It sat on my bookshelf, taunting me with a shiny invitation.

I remembered how Geepa had never gone anywhere without the pouch tucked in his shirt pocket.

I remembered what he told me the last day we were together. He had said, "Where I'm headed, the pouch will be of no use." Now I wished I would have asked more questions. It almost seemed as if he knew that he was going to die. "Money talks, kiddo; you've got to learn to listen." Geepa had told me that more than once, but I never understood what he meant. "Someday you'll understand," he would always happily add.

Giving in to my curiosity, I jumped up and reached for the coin pouch. I held it tight and sat cross-legged on my bed, staring at it. I had no idea if there were coins in there—and if so, how many. Propping my pillows behind me, I studied the pouch. It was made of soft, worn leather. I could barely make out three trees stamped into its surface. The one in the middle was taller than the others. I rubbed my thumb across the front of it. Holding it close to my nose, I sniffed. It smelled like Geepa, and that made me smile. I was a little afraid to open it. I held my breath and slowly eased the clasps open, then quickly closed it—I heard voices.

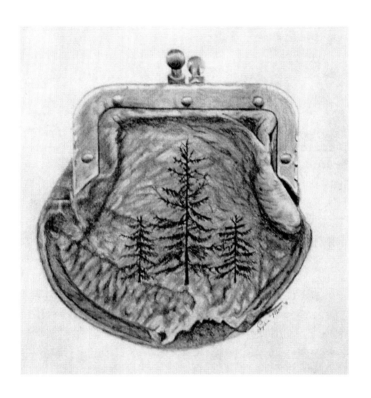

Chapter 2

Voices

*T*he voices sounded like they were coming from the pouch, but that seemed crazy. I wanted to make sure that I wasn't going loco, so I went to my bedroom door and cracked it open to see if anyone was in the hall. I could barely hear Mama and Dad talking in the kitchen downstairs, but I couldn't make out what they were saying. I quietly closed and locked my door and then propped myself back on the pillows. Holding the pouch with both hands, I opened it again, only to hear the same voices—now quieter. I looked around my room and listened carefully: no one lived in our house but the three of us. A creepy feeling came over me as I slowly looked down at the pouch. The whispering had quieted down … but I was sure that whatever was in there … was talking.

Brandon Wilks, one of the toughest guys in my school, had once accused me of being a coward. It took a punch to his face, a bloody nose, and a trip to the principal's office to prove to him and everybody else that I wasn't. Now though, I had to convince *myself.*

Slowly, I peeked in: "Who's there?"

There was no answer.

"Say something."

I opened the pouch a bit wider and carefully placed it to my ear.

"She's safe, don't be so afraid! You're acting like a child," whispered a woman's voice.

"I ain't afraid of nothin', lady," replied a man's angry whisper.

I was holding the pouch still, breathlessly waiting for more.

"She's Oliver's granddaughter; we can trust her," whispered another voice.

I was more puzzled than ever. Whoever they were, they knew Geepa and they knew I belonged to him.

"Oli's my name," I whispered into the pouch, "named after Geepa."

The silence suddenly broke. A man's voice shouted, "Where's Oliver; we wanna know what'cha done with 'im, girl!"

I nearly dropped the pouch, first from shock, then from the shout to my ear.

It's not very often someone yells at me without me yelling back, but this time it was different. Maybe, whatever was in that pouch wasn't money at all. Could they be the smallest people ever known to man?

"I didn't do anything to Geepa! He died all on his own, two weeks ago. Besides, I would never hurt him. How could you think that?" I didn't like the way this introduction was going. Whoever these voices were, they didn't know much about having good manners or making friends.

"Hey, kiddo, it's okay. Why don't you tell us about

what's happened," said a woman's kind voice from inside the pouch.

It was all so strange to me—people so small, living in a coin pouch—and someone I'd never met calling me *kiddo,* which was Geepa's nickname for me. Talking about Geepa's death made me feel sick, but I had questions of my own that I wanted answered, and all of them were about the talking people inside Geepa's coin pouch. I sat up and opened it wide. Looking in, I saw only little shimmers of reflected light.

"What are you?" I quietly asked.

"We're coins; what else would we be?"

As if it was not enough to hear voices from inside a coin pouch, discovering they were talking coins was really over the edge. I needed to know more: "Can I take you out?"

"I ain't comin' out, and you can't make me, kid," said the gruff man, who by now I had guessed to be a bully like Brandon Wilks.

"Aw, sure we'll come out, and then we can all talk about what's happened and what will come of us," said the lady's kind voice.

"I said I ain't comin' out!" Actually the bully sounded much worse than Brandon.

"My name is Penny," said the lady kindly. "Do you know what a penny looks like, Oli?"

"Well, of course I do."

"Then take me out first."

I wondered if I should do this. What kind of creature could this talking coin-thing be? Maybe, they would run away—or worse yet become huge once they were out of the pouch. Hiding big coin creatures in my room could be a real problem. And what if they needed food? What if *I* was to be their food? I decided I needed to know more before taking them out of Geepa's pouch.

"So, you say you knew Geepa. Did he know about you?" I asked them all.

"Yes, he did," answered the lady who I figured to be Penny.

"Well, if that's true, then why did he give you to me without telling you where he was going?"

"You gotta know how your Grandpa worked, kid," another man's voice spoke.

Then the other man, the gruff one, spoke: "If he knew there was somethin' wrong with himself, he never told a soul. So, what happened to 'im, kid?"

"I'll tell you, but you've got tell me something first."

"Depends what it is, kid," he said.

"Do you get big once you're out of this pouch?"

"That's crazy. If we got big when we were let out, then why would we still be here?" he answered.

"We needed your Grandpa to look after us because we're small, you know, coins," Penny said.

"Well, who's going to look after you now?" I was as curious about their fate as they were.

"Hey, Sherlock, that's a brilliant question! I'm figuring if he gave us to you, then he was hoping you would."

"*ME?*" Panic struck. It was one thing to babysit the Peavey girls, but taking care of talking coins, that was something else. Suddenly I found myself in a mess, but now I knew too much to ignore them. I had to figure out what they were and how a person was to take care of them. Besides, they wanted to know what happened to Geepa, and I promised them an answer.

"How do I grab you?" I asked as I peered into the pouch.

"Gently," said the lady's kind voice.

Chapter 3

Penny and Buck

*H*olding the pouch in my left hand, I looked in but could only see the copper coin. Reaching in, I carefully squeezed the penny and brought her out. Gasps came from the other coins inside.

"I'm not going to hurt her."

If there's any way I could have handled her more carefully, it would have been to not touch her at all. Placing her on my pillow, I squinted my eyes and stared. Head up and full of life, she stared back at me.

"Wow, that's amazing! You are a penny, but a lot more." The question suddenly occurred to me: how many other coins in the world were more than just money?

Her legs were long and skinny. In the middle of each leg was a knobby knee that looked like a small gum ball. Her arms and elbows were a match to her legs, just shorter. Without touching her legs, I could only guess they were covered in the tiniest pair of green stockings ever made. Her hair was a long, thick, tangled mess, like a spool of copper wire that had been snarled in a hair brush.

Now, I'm not the queen of great hair days, but

I knew right off, I'd need to help her out in the combing and de-tangling department. Hair care was not my specialty, which was why my blonde hair was cut in a short bob, no match for the mess on Penny's head. What I guessed to be her body was stamped with all the markings of a copper penny: Abraham Lincoln's face, IN GOD WE TRUST, LIBERTY, and 1958. It was her face that most surprised me though; her green eyes and long slender nose were like those of some of the ladies I saw in Mama's beauty magazines. Her lips were small, plump, and red.

I nearly jumped out of my pajamas when she sat up and began rubbing her legs.

"My legs get so cramped in that little pouch, and on warm days, I feel like I'm sitting in a sauna."

My mouth dropped open so wide that you could have seen straight through to my toes. I lost my words for a moment, which for a girl like me doesn't happen very often.

"Tell us what happened to Oliver," Penny insisted, staring directly into my eyes.

The thought of talking about Geepa dying made me sick, but I mustered up the courage to explain how he died. Before I did though, I threw in the notion that I thought he was in heaven and probably watching us right now. I couldn't be sure about those details and told her that I would get the heaven story straightened out from Mama and explain it later. Penny pulled her knees up in front of her, resting her chin in her hands as the tiniest of tears fell from her small face.

"I believe he's watching us," Penny said sadly, "at least that's what I'm going to believe, so if your

Mama says differently, I don't want to know." She tried to catch another tear before it fell to the pillow. "Well, go ahead, tell us what happened."

I went on to explain how Pin-e-wah, Geepa's best friend, found him on his bathroom floor and called Mama and Dad to come over, and how the people in the ambulance came and said he'd been dead for a while, probably from a heart attack. I didn't leave any of the details out because I didn't want to answer any questions when I was finished. Just once through and that would be it, forever, no more telling the story.

"I've cried every day since then, and I hope we don't have to talk about it anymore."

Not a word was spoken, but I could hear quiet sniffles from inside the pouch. Penny, looking down, straightened her legs and smoothed her tights. "Then I guess it's time to stop crying," she said, finally breaking the silence. She bent her tiny legs in a cross-legged fashion and quickly wiped her eyes. "It's normal to be sad, but then the time comes to stop," she added looking straight at me.

Oddly enough, that's exactly what I did. At that very minute, it was like she called the order, and I knew that it was right to obey, and I just chose to stop feeling sad too.

"You know this whole idea of talking to a penny is kind of weird. I'm not crazy, am I?"

"You're not crazy, Oli. Money talks, you just have to learn to listen."

I had another one of those moments where words just didn't show up. After a long pause I said in amazement, "That's what Geepa used to say."

She smiled and nodded her head. "I know, where do you think he heard it?"

There was movement in the direction of the pouch. Both Penny and I saw it at the same time. She started to stand on her wobbly legs.

"Don't move, Penny," I insisted.

I wasn't sure what to do first, make sure Penny didn't run off, or find the other coin that had crawled out from the pouch. It was hiding somewhere in the many blankets on my bed. And then, I saw it. There was no way that I could have missed the bright-colored ball; it was the head of another coin. A brightly colored-bandana covered this coin's head, a print of tropical flowers that was tied in a knot to the back. Without warning, it jumped from hiding and took off running towards the end of my bed.

As best I could see, its legs seemed strong and sturdy, but they were covered with camouflage pants. From a distance, it looked like the coin was wearing cowboy boots. When it disappeared from sight, I couldn't help but follow. Once close enough, I detected that it was a man-coin. My guess was it was the mean one. He seemed like he could have been a soldier or some guy who was in the Special Forces, like an Army Ranger, someone who was ready in a second to fight. He made a calculated dive for one of the folds in the blanket as though he was under attack. He took cover with only the top of his bandana showing. His head bounced up and down, looking like a bright-colored buoy bobbing around in an ocean of multi-colored blankets.

"Why are you hiding?" I asked him.

Then I saw his face for the first time. His brown eyes were huge. He was attractive, not that I spend my time looking at boys, but I'm at least enough of a girl to know when a boy's face looks nice.

"Whatcha think you're doing staring at me like that, girl, you sizing me up to take me hostage?"

"No, I don't plan on taking any hostages," I answered in defense.

"And how would I know that?" he fired back.

I looked at Penny with panic, wondering how

I would prove myself to a complete stranger. She must have read my mind and came to the rescue.

"For crying in the night, Buck, she's Oliver's family. Now come out from behind that blanket and show some manners," she insisted, now standing on my pillow.

He slowly worked his way out from behind the covers, but still acted as though I was the enemy.

"I'm Buck, just plain and simple. Buck." He was a glistening silver dollar.

"I'm Oli, just plain and simple. Oli."

Just as I was about to turn my attention back to Penny, there was a knock at the door. I nearly jumped out of my skin. My first thought was to herd the two back into the coin pouch, but they had plans of their own. Before I could say a word, they ran in two different directions. Not knowing what to do next, I ran to the door.

"Who is it?"

"Oli, please open your door."

"Just a minute. Let me get dressed," I asked, hoping for some time.

"Open the door now!" Mama demanded.

"Can you just give me a second?" I was desperate, stalling for just a few extra minutes to collect the coins—and myself.

"Olivia Marie Swank, you've locked yourself away in this room long enough. No more excuses. Open this door immediately."

I slowly opened the door wide enough to let her see my face.

"What are doing in there, Oli?"

"Nothin'. Just cleaning my room."

I knew it was a lie, but in a desperate moment, it had to do. Besides, I couldn't let Mama see my discovery. I couldn't be sure of what she might do.

"I have breakfast ready for you downstairs," she quietly stated, as she stole a glance into my room.

She had bought into my lie, and I was never so thankful for Mama's trusting nature. For just a second, I felt bad about lying, but then I slammed the door in her face and raced to find the coins. Realizing what I had just done, I hollered back towards the door, "I'll be right down, I promise!"

I began the rescue mission for Buck and Penny, but I couldn't find them anywhere. I made quiet pleading calls for them, but they wouldn't answer. I wondered if there were others in the pouch, but after looking, I realized if there were more, they had all gone missing.

Mama wouldn't take any more excuses, and I was expected at the breakfast table. Needing a quick solution, I searched my room and saw yesterday's bath towel lying on the floor. I threw my wrinkled jeans and dirty t-shirt on and slammed the door, tucking the towel under it. I was careful to make sure that there were no escape routes. Turning toward the staircase, I looked to make sure Mama wasn't watching.

My typical trip down the stairs was by way of the hand railing, one of the only good things about the over-sized mansion Dad insisted on living in. By the time I was eight and tall enough to slide down the railing, I never walked down the stairs again, until this morning, the morning Geepa's pouch talked.

Chapter 4

Tension at the Table

*M*ama met me at the bottom of the stairs looking puzzled.

"You didn't slide down the railing this morning?"

"Forgot," I said as I tried on a fake smile.

I followed her into the kitchen, but then, stopped dead in my tracks.

There he sat. I studied his figure sitting at the table. The starch of his pressed white shirt made him sit straight and tall while the bleached white napkin draped across his lap made him look like half of a freshly painted window frame against the dark cranberry-red wall of our kitchen.

"Hm Mmmm. Why are just standing there?"

He made me jump in surprise, startled from my trance.

"What," I snapped.

Why are you staring at me?" He looked down his nose at me, past his glasses.

"Whatever," I muttered quietly, moving towards my chair at the table.

"Well, are you going to sit down?" he asked in disgust. Pushing the glasses back up his nose, he returned to his *Wall Street Journal,* studying the small print on its pages.

"How can you even see those tiny little numbers?" I snarled.

"Sit down and eat," he ordered.

"What are *you* doing here, anyway?" My rude question stirred his anger.

"Olivia, in case you haven't noticed, I live here. This is *my* home, your mother is *my* wife, and I am *your* father. This is *my* breakfast table, *my* coffee, and *my* paper. And since when do I need *your* permission to eat breakfast at *my* table?"

"Oh, well, you don't normally eat with us," I retreated quietly.

"Sit down and eat, Olivia," he stated firmly, as he peered at me over the top of his paper.

I did exactly as I was told.

"The Dow fell again today, Abby."

"Dear, you know you shouldn't put your trust in the Dow Industrials." Mama had a way of speaking kindly to him that amazed me. How she did it I'd never understand.

"Abby, don't start that whole trust lecture with me," he replied. Mama's shoulders dropped, and she looked away, seeming to be interested in the morning dove cooing softly in the tree outside the kitchen window. Slowly turning back to me she struggled with a smile and gently squeezed my hand.

"I made your favorite breakfast, Oli. Eat up."

I sat staring into my bowl of hot cereal and blueberries, making paths around the lumps with my spoon.

"Olivia, we're all sad about Grandpa, but you've got to stop locking yourself in your room and move on with life." Once again, Dad was looking down at me over the top of his paper. His version of sad was a falling stock market. His heart was full of ice and his head full of facts and numbers. He was always ready to move on in life, but for him, on was up, and up meant more money.

"How do you know what sad feels like?" I mumbled back at him, not looking up.

"Olivia Marie, don't you speak to your father like that."

I figured Mama had to get her pitch in, too, so I let her and then returned to the network of paths in my hot cereal, carefully placing a fresh blueberry on each lump. I had nothing else to say to them. I was angry that Geepa was dead, and all I was left with was his son. It was even worse that he was my dad. Why couldn't it have been just the opposite, I wondered. Why didn't Dad die?

Geepa was different from Dad. They were alike in some ways, they both were men with the same last name, and they both had a lot of money. Like me though, Geepa didn't care about money. He lived in a small house, the same one he had lived in when he married Grandma. She died a long time ago. Geepa owned an empire of grocery stores. What started in our little town in Northern Idaho as a small store grew to chain of sixteen stores all over the Northwest. Once we moved here, Geepa sold the stores, so he could spend time with me. We spent all our Saturdays together.

Most of that time was spent at Cardboard City, a ramshackle house and two barns Geepa bought five years ago. He bought them as a shelter for homeless people living in our area. He wanted to give them a place to live where they could be fed and get out of the weather. Together Geepa, Pine-e-wah and Ben – Pine-e-wah's grandson and my best friend – and I would take food from Geepa's grocery store to Cardboard City to feed the homeless people.

I liked being with Geepa. He was simple, and I loved that about him. On Saturdays, before we would leave for Cardboard City, he would tell me to put on my work duds, which were exactly the clothes Dad scolded me for wearing. Funny how clothes can change the way you feel. When I wore my work duds, I felt as free as a bird.

Mama broke the silence: "How odd none of us saw Grandpa's death coming." She startled me so bad I nearly threw my spoonful of oatmeal and blueberries in her lap. I sat there wondering if I should say something about my last Saturday with him.

Being the kind of girl who usually said the wrong thing at the wrong time in the wrong way (and way too much) I blurted out, "I should have known, especially after Geepa gave me his coin pouch."

In anger or shock—I couldn't tell for sure—Dad slammed his cappuccino cup down in the saucer with a such loud clatter that Mama jumped, hitting her knees on the bottom of the kitchen table and knocking my full glass of grape juice over. Six hands from three directions all at once grabbed for the juice glass, knocking it into the air. Juice splattered everywhere in our huge kitchen, but most of it landed right in Dad's lap. His freshly pressed white dress shirt looked like something from a crime scene.

"He gave you that stupid coin pouch!" he shouted.

Mama and I looked at each other in fear as Dad walked to the sink, grabbing the kitchen towel, trying to blot the juice from his shirt. I didn't know what to say, which again was unlike me. He threw the towel into the sink and turned to leave the room.

"Great! That's just great," he scolded me, looking at me with disgust. "Another crazy one," he murmured, leaving the kitchen.

"Crazy? What are you talking about?" I yelled.

Mama grabbed my hand, and we sat in silence, listening as Dad quickly stomped up the enormous stone staircase. His shoes clicked on each cold marble step; we could hear him as he turned down the hallway toward his office.

Slam. The door closed angrily with a final crash. Mama and I turned to look at each other.

"What was all that about?" I asked.

"I don't know, Oli." And with that she shoved her chair back and began the job of cleaning bright purple off every flat surface in the room.

"Mama … I think I should tell you about the last Saturday I spent with Geepa. You know … the night he died."

She stopped her scrubbing and stared curiously at me. "Well, you must know something I don't, so yes. I think you should." She leaned back on her heels and rested her hands in her lap.

Chapter 5

The Last Saturday

I was a little late meeting Geepa the last Saturday I spent with him. I'd had some trouble finding my pocket knife, which was buried between the layers of candy and cookie wrappers on the desk in my room. But when I finally met Geepa, he was waiting on the street corner for me. We had to walk fast in order to reach the bus stop, and there was already a line.

We waited only a few minutes before the bus came. As it approached, I could see the driver was Earl. He was the only driver I didn't like. Geepa thought he was nice, but he would, since he never met a person he didn't like. Earl gave me the creeps though. The long scar on his face reached from ear to ear and would turn dark purple when the weather was cold. When he spoke, his voice was low and growly. His sentences were short; more than a few words would have been considered a long conversation for him. He had a sloppy cough that he was proud of. When he coughed, he'd say, 'That was a good one.' It was gross and made me sick. Like anyone cared how much stuff he coughed up.

We got on the bus, and Geepa gave Earl a pat on

the back as he dropped the money in the toll box. "Hello, Earl, how's your Saturday?"

I moved past him as fast as I could, keeping space between us.

Geepa and I sat on the bus talking about his projects for the day and the journey that I was planning into the dangerous dark woods with Ben. I explained to him that my pocket knife was safely hidden in my backpack.

"Oli, you are probably the bravest girl I know. Who else would face such dangers with only a pocket knife?" He spoke quietly to me so that none of the other people on the bus would hear that I was armed with a weapon. I smiled knowing he was really making fun of me.

We were the only two left on the bus when it slowed for the last stop.

"Well, Oliver, I guess this'll do it for you and the kid," Earl shouted back to Geepa.

"And what about you, Earl, where to from here?" Geepa hollered back.

"Back to the start, do it all over again."

I knew better than to ask Geepa why he was always so friendly to such a creepy guy. There were no creeps to Geepa. No matter how bad a person was, even the most awful person, Geepa would say, "Someone's got to love 'em, kiddo." I was glad he didn't expect *me* to love Earl.

On my way out, I rushed past Earl as quick as I could, jumping from the top step to the ditch next to the road.

Geepa wished him well, patted him on the back,

and like always said, "Keep up the good work, friend." He carefully stepped out of the bus and joined me on the gravel road that led to Pine-e-wah's farm and my friend Ben.

As we walked, I told him all about my week at school and how much I liked my new teacher. I told him that even though I liked school, I still wished that I could stay with him every day. He laughed and put his arm around my shoulders.

"I wish that you could spend every day with me, too, Oli, but I wouldn't want an ignorant grand-daughter. School gives you the tools that you need to survive, and I want you to do well in life," he explained.

The rest of the way was quiet; I just stared at Geepa's feet. He hummed a song I'd heard before and the heels of his shoes firmly crunched on the gravel road. It was a sound I'd come to love, the sound of adventure.

As we came near Ben and Pine-e-wah's house, Ben came running from the barn towards us with arms waving and yelling. Running alongside him were his two dogs, Tina and Shorty. Between the barking and yelling, I could barely make out something about a calf. I knew in an instant that Little Lady Louise (we called her Elles for short) had finally given birth to her calf.

The little creature still had signs of white sticky stuff on her, so I knew the delivery was recent. Ben was so excited that I could hardly understand him. Geepa and Pine-e-wah joined us as we stood around the proud cow, laughing as the calf tried to stand on her wobbly legs. Geepa was anxious to go to Cardboard City, so Pine-e-wah made sure Elles had plenty of hay for the day and the calf was nursing. Then the six of us—Tina and Shorty included—left for the walk over Paradise Ridge to Cardboard City.

Geepa and Pine-e-wah spent the day fixing the roof on part of the house that had fallen in under the weight of last winter's snow. While our grandpas worked on the house, we spent the day exploring and trying to find the beavers that had recently built a new dam in the creek behind the barn.

Saturdays always passed by way too fast. Ben and I were working on a beaver-proof bridge wide enough for one of us and a dog to cross over together. We were far from finishing the job when we heard Pine-e-wah holler from the house. It meant the day was over and I would have to return to town.

If I could only live in the country near Ben! We could explore every day. The city life I lived and the country life I longed for were opposites. It wasn't just Ben's friendship that I missed when I went home; it was the freedom I felt to be myself. I was full of life while at Cardboard City. Not only could I explore and listen to other people's stories of adventure, but I could also help people. Those who came to Cardboard City were the fortunate ones, the people who owned nothing but had everything. At least to me they had everything.

Ben and I made our way back to the house. Geepa and Pine-e-wah were waiting for us. Geepa was tired and asked that we not return to Pine-e-wah's farm over Paradise Ridge, the way we had come, but instead on the flat gravel road.

When we arrived, Ben and I sat on the grass under the shade of the enormous willow tree, making our plans to finish the bridge at Cardboard City the next week. Geepa went in the house with Pine-e-wah for a drink of water and a short rest. When he was ready to go, we said goodbye and began walking toward the bus stop.

I noticed Geepa was tired and looked sick. I asked him if he was all right.

"Strength is for service, not status," he explained. "Human beings are to help one another; it's what our strength is for. Promise me you will remember that, Oli."

We changed the subject to the beavers, which I was glad to talk about.

The next thing he did surprised me: he took his coin pouch from his shirt pocket.

"Oli, I want you to have this."

"But I can't take that from you," I said. "It's the pouch you've had since...well, as long as I can remember."

"On my next journey, I won't need my coin pouch," he explained.

"A journey! May I go?" I was so excited.

He looked at me kindly. "Afraid not, Oli. This one I'll do alone." His voice had a strange sound, and it gave me chills.

I looked up at him with worry, but he just smiled and handed me the coin pouch.

"You know, money talks, kiddo. You've just got to learn to listen."

The rest of the walk was quiet except for the sound of Geepa's shoes and the song he hummed.

On the bus ride home, we talked about the coming winter and the work to be accomplished at Cardboard City; it was a return trip just like all the others. He seemed more rested as he sat on the bus. After a long silence, I glanced up and saw the familiar smile on his face.

"I have that Fourth of July feeling right now, Oli." I knew all too well what would follow.

"Who gets the blessing?" I asked.

"Earl."

I looked away, hoping he wouldn't see my look of disgust.

The Fourth of July feeling was something that I never experienced before but wished I could. Geepa said when it happened, he felt the way that he did as a young boy on the Fourth of July right before the fireworks went off. A smile would explode on his face, and sometimes he would even laugh out loud. There was a joy about him that was contagious. He said that it was a gift from heaven that was meant to be shared, so he did.

"Lucky Earl," I muttered, secretly wishing it was me.

His smile grew so wide that it slipped all the way over to my face. We chuckled.

I would usually have dinner with Geepa on Saturdays, but this Saturday, I had to return home because the Peaveys were coming for dinner, and I had to watch Paige and Payton. I didn't mind Payton. She was cute, happy, and easily entertained, but Paige was different. Paige was four going on twelve, and she made it her business to tell me mine. I had my ways though. She may have been bossy, but she was also a coward. At the first suggestion of time-out in a dark closet, she was like putty in my hands.

My babysitting job with the Peavey girls meant I couldn't go with Geepa. We decided that it was a rotten deal that I had to spend my night rounding up small children, but Geepa said that their parents would be happy to have my help.

The strangest feeling came over me—like home-sickness—when I left Geepa that afternoon. It was hard for me to say goodbye. He must have felt it, too, because he hugged me longer than usual, and I'm quite sure that he was crying when he walked away.

I thought about that moment as I looked at my Mama.

She was still in the same kneeling position, staring at me with her hands in her lap, clutching the brightly stained purple wash cloth, her small body resting on her heels. I felt bad, like I should have told her before. Maybe, it would have helped.

"If I had told you Geepa wasn't feeling good, maybe he wouldn't have died." I panicked at the thought that I could possibly have stopped this horrible thing from happening.

"No, Oli! I don't ever want you to feel like it was your fault. If Grandpa wanted help, he would have asked. No, I think he might have known that it was time; maybe, there was a part of him that wanted to stay, at least for you, but, then the rest of him was tired and ready to go."

She dropped her head, and I watched as the pool of dark purple juice on the floor splashed and whirl-pooled from her tears.

Mama finally sat up and looked into my eyes as she wiped her face. "Oli, I want you to keep the coin pouch in your room. For now, that is."

"The coin pouch!" I yelled.

I remembered what I had left in my room and panicked. I jumped from the table with such an explosion, the chair shot out from behind me. I ran from the kitchen like the house was on fire. Jumping three steps at a time, I reached the top of the staircase and dove for my bedroom door. Bursting in, I gasped for breath as I slammed the door behind me and pushed the lock.

Chapter 6

Peace Talks

*W*hen my 85-pound body barged through the bedroom door, it made quite a ruckus. When you're less than an inch and under an ounce, like Buck and Penny, that kind of entry sends you scurrying for cover.

"Penny?"

"Buck?"

Not a whisper could be heard.

What if they had escaped? Was I not careful enough about plugging the cracks? My concern turned to panic. "Please, Penny! Buck, answer me." But there was nothing but complete silence. I crawled on my hands and knees, moving carefully until I reached my bed, where I had left them.

"Penny, Buck, I'm really sorry for rushing out of here so quickly. Mama was suspicious, and I couldn't make up another lie to hold her off. I hope you'll understand. Maybe, you've never had parents; maybe, you don't know how mad they get when you lie; maybe, you've never even lied before. When you're a person, though, you have all these things to think about."

I hoped that they would understand why I had to

obey Mama. Life as a coin had to be pretty simple. My life as a twelve-year-old-only-child-to-a-mom-who-worried-about-everything *had* to be harder than being a talking coin.

There was only silence.

I searched the room again, looking for any sign of shiny movement. I waited, crouched down on all fours. At last from the far corner of the bed near the wall, I heard a faint voice. Then another. I really wanted to tear into the blankets and find the coins, but I figured I'd already done enough damage. "Please come out and talk to me."

I saw a shiny reflection and a small hand grabbing the fold in the blanket.

It was the smallest hand that I had ever seen, and it was followed by a small arm, then another small hand followed by another small arm. The top of an old man's hat appeared, like the one Geepa wore over his bald head. The coin made its way to the top of the fold and plopped himself down, studying me closely. I returned the stare. He was a dime, a shiny one. Clearing his throat, he spoke in a voice like someone I'd heard on the Travel Channel.

"Bonjour, Mademoiselle Oli. I am Dimeon."

He was french, with an accent on stuffy, I thought. We stared at one another wondering who would speak next.

Underneath his thick, silver moustache, I could barely see the glimpse of a smile. "Mademoiselle, the others are well, I am pleased to report. Speaking to you on their behalf, I must say they are frightened by your abrupt movements and haste. However, we know you are in a peculiar situation and are therefore willing to act graciously and kindly toward you."

I recognized only half of the words he spoke.

"What the heck ya'll think you're doin'! Ain't nobody speaking on my behalf," shouted an angry voice from under the bed.

I recognized it in a second. "Buck, you're still here!"

Face down on the floor, I reached under the bed. Realizing that I had no idea where he was, I quickly pulled my arm back. I didn't know Buck very well, but I suspected enough to know that he wasn't about to be caught. I changed my strategy. Sitting back on my heels, I sarcastically snapped back at him, challenging his rudeness. "What did you want me to do, Buck, have Mama come in, so you can meet her?"

It was dead quiet for a second.

It was Penny who once again came to the rescue with the voice of reason in the middle of a heated moment. "Now just a minute. Before we all get into a big fight, let's come out from hiding and talk this through."I was flooded with relief to hear Penny's voice.

I remembered how Geepa and Pin-e-wah would always suggest to Ben and me that we should sit in a circle whenever an argument broke out between us. It was their approach to 'peace talks,' as they called it. Remembering this, I suggested it to the coins.

I slowly crawled to the middle of the room and reached for my climbing gear. "Okay, I'm going to take this rope and make a circle on the floor. Let's all sit around the circle and have a peace talk."

"Peace talks! Peace talks!" Buck ran out from under the bed with his fists shaking in anger. "I'll give you a peace talk, girl. I'll give you a piece of this fist right alongside your head," he shouted.

I watched the parade of coins moving across the room. Buck led the way with his fists shaking and angry words flying. Penny followed with a not so very happy look on her face. Dimeon brought up the rear with his distinguished stride and perfect posture. His legs were covered in dress pants with creases that would have made Dad proud. His arms were covered with light blue shirt sleeves with creases to match his pants. I wondered how he could keep the creases so perfect living in that cramped coin pouch.

I took my place in the circle while the others marched across the room. This would be some kind of a peace treaty, I thought to myself. I had my work cut out for me.

I heard a stirring from the corner of the bed where Dimeon had been hiding. The sun was shining directly on the wall behind my bed, casting a shadow of the window panes in a perfect gridded pattern. I strained my eyes to see what the noise might be when I saw two other glimmering objects shining in the sunlight. Buck's hollering faded in the background while I strained to hear the voices.

"Come on, Nicolette, get out here! If there's a fight to win, we'd better all be in it," said the rowdy voice of another coin coming out of hiding.

"There's no sense hidin' up there, you two. If we're gonna survive, then we gotta talk some sense into this kid," yelled Buck at the two stragglers.

More coins, I thought to myself. This is trouble. There's too many to take care of. And how many more were hiding in my room? One of the coins jumped over the blankets and looked for its path of descent. The remaining coin stood as still as a statue.

"Should I help them?" I asked Penny.

"Only Nicolette will need help," she said as I watched the other coin scale my bedpost and shimmy down with perfect form and amazing speed. His strength was incredible for a small coin. He leapt gracefully from the bed frame. I could now see he was a quarter. I watched him as he ran toward the circle.

"What's your name?" I asked him.

"Two Bits," he snapped back sharply. His thick black hair was slicked back with the shine of Brylcreem, and his sleeves were rolled up to expose rippling muscles. He wore dark sandals that reminded me of the kind on Jesus' feet, and he wore blue jeans that were frayed on the bottom, frays long enough to leave a dusted path on the floor behind him.

"You gonna pick a fight with us, kid?" Two Bits' eyes nearly drilled a hole through me and made me feel uneasy about him.

"No, I don't want to fight with any of you. These are supposed to be peace talks."

"Oli, please help Nicolette," Penny reminded me, pointing to the bed. I slowly got up and moved to the side of the bed, bending down to study her. She was a chubby little lady, her arms dressed in printed puff sleeves that reminded me of kitchen curtains hanging in Geepa's windows. She wore a slick-shiny scarf that was tightly tied under her chin. Her chubby legs were covered in stockings that I think were supposed to look like the color of skin, but were much lighter than any skin I'd ever seen. I would have guessed that she was someone's Grandma, if I thought coins could have families.

I didn't want to risk any more trouble, so I did as I was told and gently extended the palm of my hand, offering her a seat on my thumb. As I brought her closer to my face, I could see her small wire-rimmed glasses and her rosy cheeks. She backed away from me, and I realized she could fall from my hands, so I backed off.

"Hello there. I'm Oli."

"I'm Nicolette," she said with a sweet but crackly old woman's voice.

"You look like you could be someone's Grandma."

"Well, thank you," she said, "but unfortunately, coins don't have grandchildren. We don't even have children, for that matter. If you need a grandma, though, I'd be glad to be yours." She grinned hugely.

I thought that would be an offer worthy of acceptance. "Okay, I'd like that."

We smiled at each other, and I knew instantly we would get along perfectly. I carefully carried her back to the circle, where I insisted that she stay in my hand during the peace talks. I could tell she was fragile, and I would need to look after her since she had trouble getting around.

I started the peace talks with a simple question: "What do I have to do to earn your trust?"

Without a second for a breath, Buck answered my question. "Well, I can tell you this much. As far as I'm concerned, Penny is too quick to trust. Oliver would've never left us exposed to the dangers of the house like you did, free to roam 'round."

Penny was quick to snap back, "Now just a minute, Buck. Oli's a good girl. She had no choice other than leave us out here in the open world. Her Mama was calling for her."

Dimeon pitched in the most sensible words that I'd heard so far. "Calm down. As I see it, we need to make some decisions; the rules have changed. Life may be different now that Oliver is gone. We've encountered a completely different living arrangement. Oliver was an adult; he was in charge of his decisions. Oli, however, is a child; she lacks the power to make up her own mind. Judging from her actions, she is an obedient girl who will not risk disobedience in order to protect us. That speaks volumes about the character of this *jeune fille*. I believe we will have to change our lifestyle in order to cooperate with this new living arrangement, and I beg to differ with you, Buck, but I agree with Penny: we are in good hands."

"So, mister smart guy, what do suppose we do to cooperate with this kid?" Two Bits hollered. He was a mean quarter with a rowdy personality and baggy pants.

I found it interesting that they were talking as if I wasn't there. They seemed to be an organized group who had learned to cooperate and survive together. As they talked between themselves, I began to learn a lot about each of their personalities and how they fit in their group. For a moment, I forgot that I was the one who called for the peace talks. But I decided

I would let them talk and make their own decisions about trust.

"Well, I, for one, think of her a little differently than just as a kid," said Dimeon. "I suggest that we do not venture away from her care when she is called out by her parents. In other words, let us not take advantage of this new found freedom. Just as she asks for permission, I suggest we do the same before we venture out and explore."

"In case you forgot, smart guy, we're ten times her age! Since when do *we* ask for permission?" said Two Bits.

"Now just a minute," Penny interrupted, "we're not going to fight. I think we should consider Dimeon's advice and change the way we make decisions. Our lives *have* changed. And have all of you forgotten about Oliver? He was the one who left us in Oli's care."

At the mention of Oliver, there was a moment of silence. It became clear to me that with Geepa, they had been a family.

Penny stood up, hurdled the small rope, and moved to the middle of the circle. "Oli, we trusted Oliver because we knew he understood how dangerous it was for us in this world. He knew coins were more likely to be spent than saved, and a coin found on the ground was more often stepped on rather than picked up. If we had gotten lost or separated from each other—or from him—it would be the end for all of us." She looked around at them, then at me. "We need each other. And we will need you."

Buck stood to his feet and pointed his finger at me, speaking with a kinder voice than I'd heard from him before. "Oliver knew there wasn't anybody that would treat us like family except for him. He knew our value—I mean real value. Not like a hundred of Penny equaled me, or five of Nicolette equaled Two Bits, but our *real* value. He knew that Penny'd always give him the truth about stuff and that Dimeon's smarter'n a whip and that I'd stick up for him to the end. He knew Nicolette would say sweet things to him when his heart was achin' and that Two Bits would keep him honest. That's the kinda value we had to him."

Although I felt as though I was the audience, I didn't feel removed enough to sense that things were beginning to take shape.

Two Bits threw in his two cents: "And something else, kid. You gotta figure out that in order to be trusted by us, you gotta put us in a safe place before you go rippin' outta here; it's pretty hard for us to close the coin pouch from the *out*side when we're on the *in*side."

"Mademoiselle Oli, life is complicated when you're as small as we. It's peculiar that people treat a ten dollar bill with care, but they will throw a coin in a wishing well to drown. Without coins, there would be no folding money, and without folding money, there would be no wealth."

Dimeon continued, "What is more important is that we have wisdom. I have been in circulation for 83 years and passed from hand to hand nearly a thousand times before I arrived in Oliver's safe possession and care. I've seen many things. Some were tragedies; some were wonders. I have learned many lessons, and I'm glad to share my thoughts, but not with just anyone—only those whom I trust. I'll not cast myself before the unwise."

It was time for me to speak. "Look guys, I'm a kid. Okay. You act like I should be just like Geepa, but he was seventy-years-old. I've told you how sorry I was for leaving you like I did. Geepa never had to answer to his Mama while you lived with him. Besides, he wouldn't have left you with me if *he* didn't trust me. So, I've got something to say about trust, too. I'm going to make some mistakes. After all, I've never babysat money before. What I know about money is that you put the big stuff in the bank and keep the small stuff in a jar. I also know money gets a lot of people in a serious trouble. It makes them think they're something real great and special if they have it, and for others who don't have it, they think it's okay to steal and kill because they want it."

I looked around at the amazing walking, talking coins in front of me. "I knew Geepa carried this pouch around and never went anywhere without it, but until today, I never knew why. You've got to give me a chance to learn how to take care of you. And you've got to trust me that I will. Can you do that?"

"Oli's right," said the squeaky voice of Nicolette. "Maybe Oliver knew that Oli needed our help as much as we need hers. I'm guessing that's why he left us with her. She's a lovely young lady. Let's give her a chance."

"Thank you." I was glad to have someone who talked simple on my side. Nickolette had begun to grow on me. I kept thinking of what a long fancy name she had.

Then I thought of how Mama told me that it wasn't proper to call old people by their first name. A change of name was in order. "Since you offered to be my grandma, may I just call you Nanny, and not Nicolette?"

"Oh, splendid!" she said through an enormous smile. "Very well dear, that will be just fine."

"Well then, let's set the rules," Penny said, once

again standing to her feet. "I'm eager to move on and forget about this rough start."

"First Rule: We are always to be returned to the pouch when you leave us," Penny calmly ordered.

"Yeah, and the Second Rule is that it ain't good enough to leave us on the floor either, kid. Ya put us back up on the shelf, out of the way of critters and people," Buck ordered.

"The Third Rule is: When we travel with you, we are to be placed in your shirt pocket," Dimeon said.

Two Bits was certain not to be left out of the rule making: "Fourth Rule is that we wanna see the world, too, so don't go cuttin' us outta the action. We're not just innocent bystanders, got it? We get a part of the action, too."

"Since Oliver left us in your charge, we have to assume it was for a reason," Penny said. "Like Nicolette and Dimeon said before, you need our wisdom and help."

"Therefore, Fifth Rule: We need to be allowed to share our opinions, even if you don't like them."

There was a pause in the discussion, and I sighed with frustration, feeling a bit overwhelmed with the new responsibility and rules. "What if I accidently forget some of the rules? Will I get yelled at and treated like an idiot?"

"We ain't going to get mad at you unless you leave us out of the pouch or on the floor," Buck promised.

"Okay, I'll do my best, but there's one thing Geepa taught me, and it's going to be my rule. Rule Six: You can't get trust without giving it. You have to trust that I will take care of you and understand my situation with Mama and Dad. Don't go getting mad just because I have to mind *their* rules, too."

"Agreed," Penny stated firmly.

"Agreed," said the others together.

"Oh, and one more thing," I said, "are there any more of you hiding in my room?"

"No, we're all here, Oli," said Penny.

"Good," I sighed with relief.

We had made our peace; a treaty had been reached.

"How should we spend our first day together?" I asked with a bit of caution.

Chapter 7

Busy Bodies

*S*ince I was a die-hard outdoor adventurer, I decided my Uncommon Cents needed to be the same. It was about the third or fourth day after I had first met them. Mama had left the house to grocery shop, and of course Dad was gone to work. The bees, birds, and dragon flies were going crazy for moisture since the summer had been long and hot. Every day for the previous two weeks I had filled the bird bath on our back porch, taking care to provide all the visiting song birds with their water supply. I suggested a trip outdoors to my Uncommon Cents, and—with the exception of Dimeon and Nanny—they all thought it was a worthy adventure.

"Leave me inside if you please, dear," Nanny said, "I prefer the cooking programs on your television to the outside heat."

"I believe I will keep Nanny company," Dimeon said. "I'm quite uncomfortable with your outdoor shenanigans. There are far too many dangers that I prefer to avoid. Have you any good books?"

I was careful to place Nanny and Dimeon in my jewelry box, which, of course, was not filled with jewelry but instead was the storage box for my fossil collection. I made plenty of room for them to sit among the fossils. I tried not to laugh out loud at the thought of my old coins sitting among fossils;... fortunately, they did not make the connection, but I sure got a kick out of it.

I turned on the Food Network channel for Nanny and opened one of my favorite books for Dimeon: *The Higher Power of Lucky*. Since I was certain that I would be alone around the house for the morning, I placed my open box of fossils on my bed with Nanny and Dimeon safely seated inside. We all agreed that it was a safe place. Should there be any surprises, they could take cover behind any of the bigger fossils.

Buck, Penny, Two Bits, and I left for the great outdoors. I knew I didn't have time to travel far, so we chose the backyard for our exploration. None of them had ever seen a bumblebee before, and I knew exactly where to find them. Kneeling on the porch in our back yard, I opened the pouch and invited them to come out and explore the flower boxes—where, I guaranteed them, they would get a great show of bumblebees.

I took for granted the things I knew about the outdoors. For example: wasps and hornets love wood, red ants are to be avoided, and sprinklers leave puddles. What I *didn't* know about the outdoors that day was that Noah, our gardener, was scheduled to work on our sprinkler system.

The bumblebee show was superb, but Penny loved their low droning buzz best. We, Penny especially, were intent watching them draw nectar from Mama's gladiolas. Penny even carefully walked along the thin board that framed the flower box, trying for the best view, when I caught a glimpse of the hornet's nest.

"Penny!" I shouted, pleading with her to stop in her tracks. It was the unexpected scream that startled her.

She jumped with fright, losing her balance, tumbling head over heels, and her snarled copper hair twisted and bent as it rubbed the flower box's edge on the way down.

Had I been just a second faster, I could have caught her. Fortunately, she fell to the side of the flower box with the soft lawn below. Buck and Two Bits were far enough away from the hornets' nest to avoid their angry attack and took cover. Penny, however, with her shiny copper hair, caught their attention.

I hurdled the flower box and ran to her rescue. Buzzing madly around her were more than fifteen cruel hornets, waiting for the perfect opportunity to attack and sting. I grabbed her, and they turned their attention to me. I ran madly around the backyard, with Penny in hand, swinging my arms like a windmill in a tornado.

Then the sprinklers went off in perfect unison. If it wasn't enough for me to have to escape the wasps, I now had to dodge all those sprinklers shooting water at me.

Noah heard my screams and came running to the backyard. "Oli! I didn't know you were back here!"

"I'm not! I mean, I'm leaving now!" I ran toward the front yard, holding Penny securely in hand and retreating to safety.

"Are you alright, Penny?" I asked in a frightened

voice.

"Yes. Wet, dizzy and a bit frazzled, but alright," she answered. "but what about Buck and Two Bits—do you have them?"

"Oh my gosh!" I yelled, turning to run again to the back yard. As I turned the corner of the house, I failed to see the large puddle of water that a faulty sprinkler had left in the yard. My legs slid out from under me as though I was sliding into second base. Penny flew up in the air as I scrambled to catch her.

Noah—I'm sure thought I had lost my mind because he stood watching me with hands on hips regarding my strange behavior with curiosity and concern.

"Penny!" I yelled, reaching for her. Like a pro, I caught her with open, cupped hands and and scrambled for the flower pot and the others. I couldn't worry about Noah and what he might see; I had to get my Uncommon Cents to safety.

Searching among the geraniums and potted ivy in the boxes, I yelled for Buck and Two Bits to come out from hiding. They came running like mad from the farthest flower box, jumping and swatting at their behinds. I wondered what in the world they were doing but didn't waste time asking. I grabbed them and bee-lined it for the back door.

Once safely inside, I looked to see if Noah was watching. He was fishing in his shirt pocket for his glasses, then quickly put them on—no doubt to see if he really just saw what he thought he saw.

"That was a close call," I breathed. I was glad for his bad eyesight as I sat down to check on Penny's condition. Buck and Two Bits leaped out onto the floor and started swatting at their behinds again as they ran in circles.

"What are you doing?" I asked.

"What are these little red things that crawl around in the dirt?" Buck yelled.

"Oh goodness. You got into a red ant hill." I answered, "Let me help."

When I had helped them kill the red ants crawling up their pants legs, I turned my attention to Penny. She was making every attempt to walk steadily and dry herself from the sprays of water.

"Geeze, oh man!" said Two Bits. "You've gotta have a strong constitution in order to survive the great outdoors!

"I'm sorry. None of those disasters were supposed to be a part of this exploration."

"No problem, Oli," Penny kindly stated. "No exploration is without its surprises."

I was glad my Cents were understanding, yet eager to endure the unexpected. We returned upstairs to my room to tell Nanny and Dimeon about the morning. To my horror as I opened my bedroom door, I saw my bed neatly made and my room spotless.

My box of fossils was not where I left it. Neither was there the sound of television or any sign of an open book. I ran for my bed and then for my bookshelf where I usually kept my box. Freshly dusted and in its place, there was my jewelry box with its lid on. I grabbed it and ran back to my bed. I tore the lid off the box to find Nanny and Dimeon huddling frightfully behind the largest fossil of my collection.

"What in the world happened?" I asked in panic.

"Does that lady always clean your room and snoop through your things?" Nanny asked quivering.

"Oh crumbles," I said in relief, "today must have been Saavy's day to work. She's our housekeeper.

"Man, talk about a bunch of busy bodies! A girl can't even have her own house to herself for a morning!" I said in disgust. I placed Dimeon and Nanny on the bed with the others, who by now, were sprawled out on my bed.

"Well, if this wasn't quite a day!" said Two Bits proudly. "Guess we've all had a taste of the action today!"

Chapter 8

History Test

*A*fter the unexpected surprises around the house, I was more careful about putting my Uncommon Cents where they were safe, and out of the view of others. My dilemma was that I needed to put them someplace that happened to be attached to me. Jeans and baggy t-shirts were a bit of a problem. Putting the pouch in my jean pockets worked fine until I sat down – then they were squished together so tight that their legs tangled and Penny's hair gouged into the other coins' faces. Very few of my t-shirts had pockets, and packing the pouch around in my hand was a hassle. Where would I carry them?

We decided a deep-sturdy-shirt-pocket was the best solution. I had to ask Mama to buy me t-shirts with pockets the next time she went shopping. In the meantime, I wore the same t-shirts until they became so dirty or smelly Mama couldn't stand to be around me. It was all she needed to make her shopping trip urgent.

If there was such a thing as a routine for a girl caring for a pouch full of Uncommon Cents, I had achieved it. Mama discovered the hardware store was the best place to buy t-shirts with pockets, and her discovery made life much easier both for me and for my Uncommon Cents. To my surprise, the pockets were deep and sturdy, as well as big, making for a secure place to carry my pouch. My Cents were as happy with their new home as I—but for different reasons, perhaps.

Two Bits and Dimeon had become especially fond of school. Truthfully, I was glad about it because I was not a big fan of sitting inside a classroom all day—it felt more like what I imagined prison might be—so knowing they were actually learning from Mrs. James made school seem worthwhile.

Mrs. James was my history teacher, and she was nowhere close to being a favorite for me. If it was possible to like or enjoy history, Mrs. James ruined it. Large women didn't bother me, but large women wearing tight pants, tennis shoes, and hair clips did. If that wasn't bad enough, her voice was enough to break glass. She thought her students would like history more if she acted it out, which is why I think she wore tennis shoes. "Traveling" from Germany to Spain, from World War I to the Spanish Revolution in one short hour took a lot of movement, especially for a large woman wearing tight pants. Two Bits and Dimeon were, nevertheless, completely charmed by her, although they would probably have thought differently had they been forced to watch her because peering out from my shirt pocket was not permitted in the Rules, they were confined to listen from inside the pouch.

"After much review, class, I believe you are ready

for your exam tomorrow. You will be testing on the two World Wars, so please be prepared to answer many questions—most of them essay questions."

Walking home from school later, I realized how much I missed Ben. "I'll bet Ben doesn't have to take history tests," I complained to Two Bits and Dimeon. I knew they were the only two paying attention in history class.

"What makes you think so?" Nanny asked curiously.

"Because home-schooling is fun. You get to do what you want."

"Really. And you know that to be a fact?"

This time I knew she was going somewhere I wouldn't like. "Well, he never complains about tests or homework or studying," I said, preparing to defend my case.

"Is Ben smart?" Penny asked. Now I knew her and Nanny were tag-teaming this argument. I regretted ever bringing the subject up.

"Yes. Ben's smart, and he knows a lot of history, but that's because Pine-e-wah tells him cool stories about his people—wars and crazy stuff that used to happen in the old days."

"Oh! Trust me Oli, if you're looking for cool stories about the old days, we've got a few of our own," Buck bragged.

"Well? Why have you been holding out?" My irritation turned to accusation.

But the history discussion became history itself as we walked through the kitchen door. We were greeted by the smell of chocolate chip cookies. Mama had a warm plate of them on the counter with a note tucked under it:

Oli,
Don't spoil dinner! I'm next door visiting Gwendolyn's mom.
3:25 p.m. Love you, Mama

Three cookies would be enough for us. I grabbed two for myself and one for my Cents, pouring a glass of milk as well. We headed for our room—history homework would have to wait—cookies, milk, and old-timer stories were next on the schedule.

"So Buck, tell me a cool story." I released them from the pouch and broke their cookie into small pieces, giving it to them.

Buck said, "I was the first dollar ever earned in Oliver's grocery store. That was back in '65 and dang if I wasn't the best of all of 'em."

"No, Buck, Oli said she wanted a *cool* story," Two Bits snapped.

"You mean Geepa saved his first dollar?" I interrupted.

"Yep. He sure did, kid."

"It seems strange that he would—but I guess he had good reason. Did he know you were a talking coin?" I asked.

"It's not the coin who decides to talk. It's the owner who decides to listen," Buck said.

The thought of money talking and owners listening had never occurred to me. *Who does Buck remind me of,* I wondered, but then it suddenly occurred to me:

Earl. He was just like Earl. Buck always had a point to make, and he got right to it. He used only a few words, but the point was made just the same.

"Before Oliver, I was passed around a few hundred times. There's only one other guy who really stands out in my mind, and not because he listened, either. His name was Franklin something...his friends called him Frankie. Best I could figure, he dealt in counterfeit money, and I don't think that made him a real popular guy even among his friends. He'd dodged the draft in '61, said he'd be hung before he fought in 'Nam—I think that was the name of a war—I haven't heard Mrs. James talk about that one yet."

Buck went on to explain how Frankie talked *to* his money—he never listened. He had two big boxes: one labeled MONEY, and the other labeled SOAP. The money he counterfeited went in the SOAP box.

"Frankie had a lot to say *to* his money, but somethin' he never learned was to listen to it and for that matter, anyone else. That came back to bite him though. One night a so-called friend walked in on him and saw he was counterfeiting money. The guy shot him square between the eyes. The murder went unsolved. Too bad nobody listens to coins; I was an eye witness. I could have given the police every detail, even the color of the shooter's shoes."

"Get out! You've gotta be kiddin' me!" My amazed response must have fueled them because there was almost a fight about who got to tell the next story. Two Bits took over.

"The day I came to Oliver, he had rushed to the hospital with his pregnant wife. He ran through the front doors where I lay staring up from the floor at the bottom of—by my count—three hundred twenty-seven pairs of shoes rushing over the top of me. Oliver stopped dead in his tracks, leaned over and stared at me, face to face. His wife was a hollerin' something about contraptions or attractions—something like that, couldn't tell for sure—but Oliver picked me up and carefully placed me in that there coin pouch. Before dropping me in, he said something about how I'd bring him good luck."

"So that must have been when Dad was born," I added.

"And I figure I did bring Oliver some good luck, in the form of your Dad."

"From what I know about your Dad, he's a pretty wealthy man, done pretty well for himself," Buck said.

"Yeah well, just 'cause a guy makes good money doesn't mean he's done well." My Cents all looked at me with surprise. If they didn't know how I felt about Dad before, they certainly did now. After moments of uncomfortable silence, Two Bits continued.

"I was the third coin in Oliver's pouch, came to him in 1964. The reason I got such strong legs is 'cause I've done some runnin', and I don't mean in races. You know how many people want a quarter just to squander? When's the last time you turned your nose up at one? Laundromats or parking meters are one thing, but I done my share of runnin' from slot machines, casinos, poker tables and the like. It's not easy being a quarter, kid, you're on the run a lot."

"Really! I never thought about it like that, Two

Bits. I mean, I always thought coins were meant to be spent. Isn't that what you're made for?"

"Yep, most folks think that. But what about us? Ya think we like being dropped into machines, drowned in wishing wells, traded for paper money? Don't we get a say about our lives?"

I realized for the first time how my Cents had become more than money to me. They had *real* value. It also occurred to me for the first time that history meant a lot more than dates, wars, deaths or countries: it was about people and their stories.

"Oli, since you're about to take a test on wars, let me tell you: I was in one," Dimeon quietly volunteered the next story. "I was minted American, raised French, and fought in wartime with the Brits. The USA pulses through my blood, and I'm stamped *In God We Trust*. My allegiances are with God first, and America second. My accent is French, but I'm marked American."

Dimeon had a way of quieting the others. He had a, "Yes sir," kind of way about him, which wasn't bad for a little dime. "You actually fought in the war?" I asked curiously.

"I speak the truth, Mademoiselle Oli. I supported my British owner who fought in the Korean Conflict. One who endures war needs courage and friendship. I was the captain of courage to anyone who knew money talked. There were those who listened. One does well to believe."

Dimeon explained he had been the first coin in Geepa's pouch, given to him by a French-speaking Briton. The man had become Geepa's close friend at the end of World War II in 1945. "The poor gent handed me to Oliver as he lay in a pool of his own blood. I believe the last words he spoke were to bequeath me to Oliver."

"Wow, that's the best war story I've heard." I stated in amazement.

"So, my dear, do you still think history is so boring?" Nanny asked curiously.

The next hour was spent talking about the travesties of war, the reasons they were fought and the heroes that died for the value of freedom. When I closed my history book that afternoon I not only felt sure I'd ace my history test, but I also felt the little history I'd learned was a part of me.

"So, if I forget an answer, can I give a shout out for help?" I asked curiously.

"No chance!" Two Bits scolded me. "The reason we've survived as long as we have is 'cause we're honest. Maybe, you think cheatin's just an everyday deal, but it ain't to us. Ya cheat once, you'll cheat twice. Before too long, it's just easy. No sir, we're gonna do just like the Rules say, we're gonna be as quiet as common cents."

Two Bits ended that discussion with no arguments from anyone. I felt embarrassed for even asking.

Chapter 9

Peanut Butter and Jelly

I wasn't one to brag, but I aced my history test. I was starting to get the hang of wars; it helped to have some history buffs living in my shirt pocket. Mrs. James, however, didn't get any easier to look at. Adults shouldn't try so hard. Well, wait a minute, maybe I'm wrong about that. If I can still remember the way that she looked and all those dates and facts about World War II then maybe she did a good job. After all, if she was hoping to leave an impression on me about history, she did.

The pains of school just dragged along. I counted down the days to summer freedom. The fact that my Uncommon Cents joined me in school helped. I never knew what it was like to have a brother or sister, but now I had five of them.

It wasn't long after they started going to school with me that I realized they hardly knew a thing about computers, cell phones, video games, or good television programs. Talk about time warping! I gave them all lessons on what was *in*, what was *out*. Geepa had never given them exposure to the awesome stuff in life—for me, that would have been a peanut butter and jelly sandwich.

We didn't often spend time in the kitchen because Mama was always there. Besides, we had tile countertops, and I knew Nanny would have a hard time navigating what to her were the ditches between tiles. Nanny, being older, had trouble on rough terrain. I would be careful to watch out for her, mostly because I wasn't sure how much a grandma could do. Judging by the grandmas I'd seen around town, they were a fragile bunch.

Nanny was interested in cooking. She really liked watching those kinds of programs on television, too, so I thought it would be good to at least try getting her into the kitchen. But it had to be when Mama was away, which was a challenge. But she worked at our church's food bank on Thursdays and usually never came home until Dad did—around six o'clock. That would be the perfect time to show Nanny around the kitchen and teach her how to make a peanut butter and jelly sandwich.

So, I explained the kitchen plan to my Uncommon Cents. Nearly all of them thought it was a great idea, except for Dimeon. He was the cautious one, always evaluating the possible dangers in every expedition we made. But the others, even Penny, the voice of reason, were excited about the idea of wandering around the kitchen. "Peanut butter and jelly sandwich?" She said. "Sounds good to me. Just make sure to keep Nanny safe around sharp objects. She falls easily."

The week crawled at a worm's pace waiting for Thursday afternoon to finally arrive. When it did, we were all totally pumped for the expedition, except for

Dimeon. I threw my backpack on the staircase and ran to the kitchen, setting the open coin pouch on the counter. With the kitchen towel hung over my left arm, I bowed and waved them out to freely roam the wonderful great plains of the kitchen counters.

"Monsieur Dimeon, may I introduce you to...Le Kitchen," I said in my best attempt at a French accent.

He was not thrilled. Smirking, he replied, "I don't like this, Mademoiselle Oli. How do you know your Mama will not come home early?"

"She's never home early. I can absolutely guarantee it. Just relax and enjoy the kitchen."

The others followed Penny in single file, stopping, staring and then walking farther only to stop and stare some more.

"Well, I can tell you one thing" said Two Bits, "I've been around enough to know a kitchen, and I'm telling you, *this* is a kitchen!"

Nanny said, "This doesn't look a thing like what I've seen on *Top Chef*. Why are there all these ditches to jump over?" She tripped and stumbled into Two Bits in front of her, causing a chain reaction. She fell on him, he fell on Buck, and Buck simply flattened Penny. Dimeon was far enough behind to escape the pile up.

Turning quickly to see the train wreck, he stated with more concern than ever, "This is not a good idea!"

"Should I call the medics?" I asked jokingly.

"We're just fine. Thanks for caring, Oli," Penny replied sarcastically. "Buck, would you please get off my hair?"

I helped Nanny first, offering assistance to the others in turn, but they all ignored me. I told Nanny that she had to let me hold her on this kitchen expedition.

"That would be best, dear," she agreed, and I picked her up

I invited everyone to explore, but I warned them to watch out for the edge of the counters, the stove, the knife rack — and most important — the sink. I explained that if they fell in, they could be lost forever. If that drain wasn't menacing enough the disposal would be a sure and swift way to death. I thought I made my point pretty well as they all turned in the opposite direction to explore. Nanny rode safely in my hand as I finished the tour of the kitchen, keeping my eyes on the others as they navigated the counter terrain.

"Why such a big kitchen for only three people?" asked Nanny.

"Ah, it's that way with Dad, everything's gotta be big and showy. I hate it. Do you know how rotten it is to be rich? Since you're all coins, I'm guessing you don't."

"Thanks for the compliment, kid," Buck rejoined, "I'm as easily a bill as a coin — and that's not poor, so don't go there with me."

Two Bits was exasperated with him. "Oh that's right. You think you're really something, Buck. You're the only one of us who could be paper, and you're always throwing that in our faces."

"Whatever! It's true, isn't it?" Buck replied.

I interrupted the argument. "I hate being rich. You don't have many true friends, only people who think they can get something from you. And when they're not using you, they're making fun of you, like those snotty girls in my class who call me Swanky. When I grow up, I'm not going to be rich. I'm going to travel the world with you five, Ben, and a backpack."

"*Tres bien, Mademoiselle*, excellent idea. It's the best you've had today," Dimeon said.

Nanny, however, was far more impressed with the tall maple cabinets that reached to the ceilings, the massive (to her) tile work on the floor and counters, and she admitted that she had never seen such an amazing kitchen. "If all one does in this room is prepare food, I would like to think you eat quite well, Oli," she said in amazement.

I sensed Nanny was anxious for the planned task. I asked her if she was prepared to start her first cooking lesson, and she answered by rubbing her hands together eagerly and smiling enormously.

I placed her carefully on the tile counter. "The first thing you have to do is make sure you have all the ingredients," I explained. Since that didn't require much effort, I simply placed the packaged loaf of bread and the jars of peanut butter and strawberry jelly on the counter.

"I'm the master of peanut butter and jelly. Trust me, creamy peanut butter and raspberry jam are the best—but because of seeds and for the sakes your small mouths, we'll use strawberry jelly today. Jelly does not have seeds, like jam, Nanny. Whole wheat bread is a must too; the jelly won't make the bread soggy if we use whole wheat." I knelt so that I could be eye level with Nanny as I explained the details to her.

I placed a butter knife on the counter and asked Nanny if she could pick it up. She eagerly bent over and attempted to grab the thick end of the knife with her arms. Grunting a bit, I could see that she was making every effort to move the knife off the counter, but it didn't budge. I realized this would be a problem with other kitchen duties as well. "Let me help you."

"I'm not what I used to be," she said with a sigh of disgust.

"These are heavy tools, Nanny. We'll just have to work together until I can find some that are more your size."

We spread the peanut butter until the bread was covered with a heavy layer of it. Nanny let go of the knife and moved as close to the bread as possible, taking care not to fall in. She rolled her sleeves up and stuck her chubby hand in the peanut butter. With a huge smile, she looked at me, not sure what to do next.

"Go ahead, try a taste," I said, coaxing her with my hands.

By now the others had stopped their own explorations and watched with anticipation from a distance. One thing I figured out with Geepa was that old people ate *really* slow. I could have eaten two meals in the time that it took Geepa to finish scooping peas on his fork, which was totally annoying. I could see that it would be no different for Nanny.

"Go ahead," I said impatiently.

Two Bits shouted from across the room, "What's the hold up, there Nickie? Tell us what it's like."

Smacking her lips, she finally gave her answer in

one word: "Delicious!"

The others then joined us. Nanny and I started spreading the jelly as we discussed the difference between strawberry jelly and raspberry jam. I was relieved that we didn't use crunchy peanut butter and wondered if I had made a bad choice with whole wheat bread.

Buck had managed to drag one of Mama's tea bags with him, using the paper tag at the end of the string as his handle. He and Penny took a seat on the tea bag as they watched me finish the sandwich construction.

I laughed to myself to see how handy they were. "A tea bag for a sofa! How smart of you, Buck! Is it comfortable?"

"You betcha. I'd like to keep this thing around, in fact. Beats sitting on the hard ground; plus, it's not too heavy," he said proudly.

"And it smells wonderful," said Penny.

They all agreed that Buck had made the find of the day, so I took another tea bag from Mama's stash and carefully placed it in the pouch.

Nanny was glowing with pride. "Who would like a taste of our peanut butter and jelly sandwich?"

"Dish it out. Looks like something I could dig my teeth into," said Two Bits, licking his lips.

I carefully had everyone move back while I used a sharp knife to cut the sandwich into small pieces. I placed one on the counter in front of each of them, suggesting they take small bites. "Peanut butter is really thick, and the jelly is sticky, so you have to eat slowly, or it'll get stuck in your throat," I explained.

They started eating their tiny sandwiches, and I

smiled with pleasure, listening to their tiny lips smack together. Their pleasure suggested that the sandwich had passed the taste test. Before I had a chance to finish my portion, they had wolfed theirs down. I looked at them in amazement. "Geeze—you guys need to eat more often?"

Two Bits said, "Yeah…and whose job would that be?"

"My best memory of food was army rations, Mademoiselle," said Dimeon, who had calmed down enough to begin to enjoy the kitchen expedition.

Penny said, "I used to eat stale bubble gum that I found lying next to me on the floor in the Five and Dime Store…gee, that's been a long time ago…must have been 1959."

Now it was Nanny's turn to speak. "One of my owners loved food…that must have been back in 1961. She was a messy little girl, and she *loved* chocolate glazed doughnuts. She handled me often enough right after eating them. I think her mother worked in a bakery and brought home the day-olds. That mother should have stopped though; her little girl was a chubby little thing who smacked her lips whether she was eating or not. I think it was just out of habit."

Two Bits said, "French fries were my favorite. They used to collect in the same pocket as me. That was back in '54, when fast cars and French fries went together."

"Absolutely awesome!" Buck licked his fingers. It was all he said.

I was glad for the expedition and the new food tastes that they'd discovered. Taking two more pieces of bread from the bag and slathering the peanut butter and jelly on as thick as I could, I invited the others to dip their fingers in and eat to their hearts' content.

A familiar sound came from behind me, and I froze.

What in the world was she doing home? I panicked. "Hey! Everybody in the pouch!" I hissed.

They laughed, thinking I was playing with them.

"No chance now," Two Bits said happily.

Mama's voice became clearer as she approached the kitchen: "Hi, Oli. You won't believe who showed up at the Food Bank today."

Then, of course, I had five coins scrambling like rodents in every direction. I had to get them into the pouch before Mama came closer. I grabbed the pouch and whispered another order: "Get in the pouch now!"

Except for Nanny, they all turned to run for the open pouch, and for a second, I was glad they were all so quick and agile. But Poor Nanny stood as still as a statue.

Mama was quickly approaching.

The coins ran single-file into the pouch, but Nanny just stood looking desperately at me for help. Without thinking, I followed my reflexes: I scooped her onto the peanut butter sandwich, concealing her with the jellied slice of bread on top. I took the sandwich in one hand and the pouch in the other, turning for the back door.

"Oli, I was talking to you," Mama said, watching me curiously.

"Ahh...I'm sorry, Mama, but I'm really late," I yelled back at her while dashing for the door.

"Late? Late for what?"

I knew that tone in her voice. Her quiet insistence meant I was to stop and answer her. But if I didn't get Nanny out of the peanut butter, she'd suffocate. I had no choice but to run.

"I'll be right back, Mama! I'm going to give this sandwich to Gwendolyn," I shouted back at her as I ran out the door.

Gwendolyn was the neighbor girl, only three and skinny as a post. Mama always said her mother was too busy with her work-from-home job to properly care for her. I knew that excuse would buy me at least five minutes, which was enough time to rescue Nanny from the sandwich predicament I had placed her in.

I was ashamed at how easily the lie slid off my tongue.

I ran around the corner of the house while looking back to see if I was safely out of sight.

I didn't see the rake Noah had propped against the corner of the house. Tripping on the tongs of the rake, I lost my balance—and the pouch. It rocketed through the air while I tightened my grip on the sandwich.

The landing was anything but pretty. My back throbbed from the pain of the tongs of the rake jabbing my skin. "The pouch!" I was desperate.

Watching it fly through the air in the direction of the basement steps, I scrambled to my knees to grab it. If I'd have been a second faster, I might have caught it.

I heard the clank of coins crashing together. I watched it as it bounced down the steps until it finally rested on the downspout.

I could hear Nanny choking from inside the sand-wich. Quickly and carefully, I removed the top slice of bread. Nanny was covered in peanut butter and jelly and gasping for air. "Nanny, I'm so sorry, are you alright?"

"I think so," she coughed and choked, trying to catch a breath of air.

Oh boy, I knew I was in for it. Dimeon would have the first word, and Mama would have the last. But I didn't care, as long as Nanny was okay.

I took her from the peanut butter and tried my best to clean her off. Her sleeves and scarf were covered in a thick gooey mess. I would have to figure out how to wash her, small as she was. Once I knew for sure she had recovered, I carefully placed her on the window ledge and made sure that she wasn't hurt.

I could hear high pitched shouts coming from the pouch. I knew I was in for a good chew-out. Bracing myself for the worst, I crawled down the steps toward my Uncommon Cents. I looked at Nanny and announced to her that I was in for it. When I opened the clasp, the first thing I saw was the colorful ban-dana on Buck's head followed by numerous hands reaching up.

A loud holler sounded from the pouch: "Yee haw!"

I looked closer to see nothing but bright eyes and beaming smiles.

"I've ridden on the back of a bucking stallion before, but that weren't nothin'. James Bond would have been impressed with your escape! Nice job kid, ya got us outta there like a pro," Buck clambered out of the pouch and jumped into my hand.

"C'est du bon, Mademoiselle!" said Dimeon excitedly, *"Tres bien*, and good job," he laughed, climbing out. I hadn't noticed the split in his white teeth before until that moment. It was probably because I'd never seen him smile so big. His moustache was messy, and his hat set sideways on his distinguished head. He laughed and jumped for my hand like a younger coin.

"Sweet ride!" said Two Bits. "That beats the heck out of a fast convertible! Pretty cool that I got a taste of PB&J, too. It ain't any better than that, is it?" He peered up at me with his hair completely disheveled and falling in his eyes. He jumped over the side of the pouch, both feet to one side, reminding me of a gymnast on the vault.

Penny said, "Oli, that was terrific! Brilliant moves, and thank you for such an amazing ride. It reminded me of a roller coaster." Never before had I seen such radiance in her face. She was strikingly beautiful at that moment.

It took me a minute to recover, but mostly from the shock of their happy reactions. I thought for sure that I was in deep trouble; instead, they'd had the time of their lives and were thankful for my quick deliverance.

Chapter 10

Making Good

"I'm glad you all liked the adventure even though the ride out was a bit abrupt." I was thrilled at the outcome of what could have been a total disaster. I was able to collect my thoughts as I continued to clean the peanut butter and jelly mess from Nanny.

"I guess you should all get back in the pouch now. I've got to go inside and deal with my lie."

"Why do you have to lie?" asked Nanny with a stern tone.

"Well, I said I was taking the sandwich to Gwendolyn, and here I sit."

One by one, they started climbing back in the pouch. I stared curiously at them as they took their places and stared back at me. Penny was the last to climb in. She turned to look at me before stepping over the clasp.

"You're not going to lie," she said firmly.

"What do you mean?"

"Carry on then, to Gwendolyn's house," Dimeon ordered.

"Oh, I didn't really mean that," I stated, defensively.

"You've got the sandwich, kid. What more do ya need?" Buck asked curiously.

"But I've never been to Gwendolyn's house before. I've only talked to her over the fence."

"No time like the present," Nanny insisted. They all stood in the pouch staring back at me.

How awkward, I thought to myself, *taking a sandwich to someone I barely know.* But I could tell there would be no further discussion, so I closed the pouch, climbed to my feet and headed for the front door of my neighbor's house—coin pouch in one hand and peanut butter and jelly sandwich in the other.

I hesitated for just a moment before I rang the doorbell at the front door. Once I did, I waited for what seemed like forever. Gwendolyn's mom finally appeared, looking completely annoyed that she had to leave her work.

She opened the door and spoke rudely. "You're the neighbor kid, aren't you?"

"Ahh. Yes, ma'am. Oli's my name. Is Gwendolyn here?"

"Gwenny, come here!" she shouted behind her, looking completely irritated.

Upon hearing Gwendolyn running for the front door, her mother turned and disappeared. *How odd,* I thought to myself, thinking the mother of a four-year-old would want to meet a stranger before she left her little child alone with her.

Bending down, I looked eye to eye with the skinny little girl. "Hi, Gwendolyn, how are you?"

"Hi. Whatcha doin' with that sandwich?" she asked, staring at my hand with the peanut butter and jelly sandwich.

"I made it for you," I said.

She stared at me like she'd never seen anything of the kind. She snatched the sandwich from my hand and nearly swallowed it without chewing.

I invited her to sit outside on her porch with me. The thought of going inside her house made me feel creepy. Besides, heaven forbid, I go inside and bother her busy and very rude mother.

I placed the pouch beside me and opened it up just enough for the coins to observe us.

"That was yummy," she said, happily licking her fingers.

We sat together and talked about all sorts of things. For a little girl, she certainly had a lot to say. As she went on, a weird feeling started coming over me. Really, it was just that I felt as happy as I could possibly be. I couldn't describe what it felt like beyond that.

I realized: It was the Fourth of July feeling.

I did what I knew Geepa would have done. Quietly, I whispered, "Blessings to you, Gwendolyn." Whether it was from Geepa or heaven, I wasn't sure—maybe both—but it felt good to pass it on. Plus, I decided if acts of kindness gave me the Fourth of July feeling, I would be doing a lot more of it.

"Well, I better get home, Gwendolyn. My Mama will wonder where I am."

"Come over again. We can play dolls," she said hopefully.

Now that's taking it too far, I thought. "How about I bring you a peanut butter and jelly sandwich again?"

"Goodie! Tomorrow?" she asked excitedly.

"I don't know about that, Gwendolyn, but I'll come over again soon." I took up my Uncommon Cents, and we started across the yard toward home.

"Pretty easy to do the right thing, ain't it kid," said Buck in his gruff voice.

"Yes, it was," I replied smiling, thinking of Geepa.

We walked in the back door, and I closed the pouch, carefully placing it in my pocket. With that, I tried to pick up where I left off with Mama. "Who did you see at the Food Bank today, Mama?"

She spun around to see that it was me. She smiled and walked over.

"Oli, I saw you sitting with Gwendolyn on her front porch. How kind of you to take her a sandwich!" She was quite enthusiastic.

We sat together in the kitchen talking about the day and those who had come from Cardboard City to visit her at the Food Bank. After that, she told me to clean up my peanut butter and jelly mess, which I was glad to do.

Closing my bedroom door behind me, I took the pouch from my pocket and opened it, sprawled out on my bed. "Ya know, … Gwendolyn's mom seems mean."

"Yep. Pretty much," Two Bits said as they all climbed out of the pouch. They were still a bit disheveled from their fall down the basement stairs.

"Do you think she sees Gwendolyn as worthless?" I asked them. "Maybe it's because she's just a little kid. Maybe, her mom thinks she's not worth her time or something like that."

"Does our age have something to do with our worth?" Nanny answered in a troubled voice.

"Well, you guys are all pretty old. What do you suppose you're worth?" I knew in a second that the words that had left my mouth sounded wrong. I felt horrible. It was something Dad would have said.

Like firecrackers on a quiet night, five small voices echoed each other:

"Worth!" said Penny.

"Worth!" said Nanny.

"Worth!" said Dimeon.

"Worth!" said Two Bits.

"Worth!" said Buck.

They all looked at each other.

Buck's sharp tone shot right through to my insides: "I don't know, kid. Whatcha suppose you'd be worth if your mom and dad decided to sell *you?*"

"I'm sorry, that was a terrible thing to say." If silence could be cut, we would have all had a big chunk.

Penny spoke. "Worth is something different to everyone. Your grandpa would have given his life for us, and that's the truth. Most other people would just pass us on the street if we were lying there staring heads-up at them. The question really is: What are we worth to you?"

I wanted to answer her, but I felt so ashamed of myself for even thinking about their worth that I couldn't say a thing. Moments of uncomfortable quiet followed. At last I lifted my head and looked at each of them. "What I meant to say was that I don't think Gwendolyn's mom thinks she's worth much ... just like I don't think Dad thinks I'm worth very much. I'd probably be worth more to him if looked and acted like he wanted me to. Ya know, a girl with long hair, pretty smells, and painted finger nails. He decides the worth of everything by how much it costs or how good it looks."

"But Mama," I continued, "now she sees me for who I am on the inside. That's how I see all of you. Even if you *are* small coins, to me you're all as worthwhile as Gwendolyn."

The *worth* conversation ended with quiet nods of agreement and relief from my Uncommon Cents. But for me, the topic of worth put a knot in my stomach and made my throat tight. Why couldn't I understand *my* worth? We would talk about worth again, but it would be a much different conversation. The exploration to the kitchen was a success, in more ways than I could count.

Chapter 11

A Surprise of the Worst Kind

Spring visited our town much earlier than it did in the mountainous regions of Northern Idaho. Daffodils in the garden usually meant that snowpack had melted to below a foot of depth in the mountains.

I loved snow for a million reasons, but Mama didn't feel the same way. It was driving in the white stuff that harried her. I hadn't been out to Ben's house or Cardboard City for nearly two months. The rub was that I couldn't get there because Mama was scared of the slippery country roads.

There was something else about spring in our town, too; it meant wandering wildlife. The foraging elk, deer, and moose became mighty hungry after Idaho's long winter, and the young shoots of spring wheat on the rolling hills of the Palouse were a tasty treat. As a result, wolf and cougar sightings would be the talk among farmers around town. On the prowl for a good meal, the predators wreaked havoc on the cattle and sheep farms, plus, they followed the young elk, deer and moose near town as if they had an open invitation for dinner.

But it wasn't just the wildlife. Avalanche risk

was high, and exploring became a bit risky during the winter and early spring seasons. Snowmobilers and skiers and hikers were warned of the dangers, often choosing the risk to add to their thrill. But outdoor adventurers like Ben and me knew that sudden changes in the weather across the rugged mountains could mean real trouble.

Gus lived in the high country, and like the wild animals, he came down from the mountains only when the deep snows and bitter cold drove him out. His house was nothing more than a shelter, so in the winter, he moved to Cardboard City.

Homelessness looked different in the rural areas than in the cities. Some of the homeless people were wanderers; they left the cold in the mountains during the winter because it became too harsh up there for them to survive. There were others, though, like Gus, who stubbornly stayed longer. Geepa called Gus and the people like him hermits. They were an offbeat kind of people. Some were dangerous, but others like Gus were friendly.

When Geepa was alive, Ben and Pine-e-wah and I would take food to Cardboard City and make sure all the homeless people were taken care of. Since Geepa never drove, Pine-e-wah would come to town on Mondays in his truck.

We loaded his old 1954 Chevy pickup—held together with bailing wire—with meat, fruits, vegetables, and day old breads. The old jalopy drove about as fast as I could walk. The four of us would drive to Cardboard City packed inside like corn kernels on a cob.

Pine-e-wah would cook a hot meal in the dingy kitchen, and then Ben and I would hand out the food. During the warmer months, the hermits would stuff their meals and any other food they could fit in their packs and head back up to their high country homes.

As I thought about Gus, I wondered if he made it down from the mountains to Cardboard City for the winter. Pine-e-wah and Ben would know, but one way or another, it was time for a visit.

I heard Mama singing in the kitchen, which was a good sign. Her good mood meant I had just the perfect opportunity to ask for a favor.

"Hey, Mama, what's up? I asked, leaning over her shoulder.

She looked suspiciously at me over the top of her reading glasses, tilting her head. She frowned. "Okay, Oli, what do you need?"

"What do you mean?" I stepped back, turning to face her.

"I know when you want something." Mama smiled as she reached for my hand.

"I really miss Ben and Pine-e-wah. I was thinking since it's not snowing anymore, and its Saturday, could I ride the bus out to their house for a visit?"

"Your dad doesn't like you going out there. He thinks it's too dangerous," she said. She closed her recipe book, so I knew this could become a tough argument.

"Mama, he doesn't even know what it's like out there. But I know how you hate driving the country roads in the winter—I could catch the eleven o'clock bus and be back before six, before Dad gets home from work."

She studied my face. "I don't know. He would be very unhappy if he found out you had gone, and even worse if he knew I had allowed it."

"Dad would never know though, I promise! I'd be back by five, have a shower and change, and he'd never know I left the house. Come on, I really miss 'em, *please* Mama. Shouldn't I check on everyone at Cardboard City anyway?" I asked.

"Well," she said, "I suppose…"

I started celebrating excitedly even before she finished.

"Since I haven't driven out there this winter … it would be good for you to go and check on things. Look in on the food supply. If we're too low, I'll have Pine-e-wah make a food run next week."

"Awesome!" I danced around the kitchen.

She smiled. "I have one of Grandpa's old pictures I'd like you to give to Pine-e-wah. I'll send it with you today. You'd just better be home by five o'clock—or there'll be a steep price to pay." Her voice was firm and commanding.

I knew I'd have to get ready fast to catch the bus. I was excited, and so were my Uncommon Cents. I knew that I'd need to dress in layers since Ben and Pine-e-wah's house was nearly the same temperature inside as outside. I also knew that we'd hike over Paradise Hill to Cardboard City, so I needed boots and plenty of sock layers in order to trudge through the snow.

I tucked the coin pouch safely in my shirt pocket and overheard my Cents making plans of their own.

"What's up, little people?" I asked, removing the

pouch from my pocket. I placed it on my desk and opened it, and they burst out in excitement.

"You're taking us, right, kid?" asked Two Bits.

"Yep! But I don't know how much you'll hear, tucked under all the layers I'm putting on."

"Can't you find a pocket on the outer layer for us?" Buck pleaded.

"Guess I could put you in the pocket of my flannels," I answered. "I think you'll be safe there." I knew all five of them were excited to visit Ben, Pine-e-wah, Gus, and Cardboard City. For them, being old souls, it would be like a walk down memory lane.

Then it suddenly occurred to me that we—my Uncommon Cents and I—had all been on the same journeys back and forth over Paradise Ridge for the last five years; they, of course, rode in Geepa's pocket. But for all this time we had never spoken to each other until five months ago.

"You had better get a move on if you plan to catch the eleven o'clock bus!" Mama called from the bottom of the stairs, her voice startling me from my thoughts.

I shooed them in, snapped the pouch shut, and tucked it in the pocket of my flannels, grabbing my hat and gloves as I ran out of my room and slid down the banister.

"Thank goodness there's only one of you," Mama said. "If I had two of you, like my Mama had your Aunt Gabby and me, I'd be doomed," she said, laughing.

Mama's twin sister Gabby was Mama's opposite. Where Mama was quiet and calm, Aunt Gabby was loud and zesty. She lived only two states away, in Colorado, but you would have thought they lived next door with as much as they talked and texted on their phones.

I put my heaviest coat on and then heaved my backpack on my back, full of survival supplies and Geepa's picture.

"You'll need money for the bus fare," Mama said. "Here's a dollar for the ride out, and the same for the ride back."

I didn't tuck the money away in my pocket, holding it carefully until the bus stop where I would listen to it before spending it. My Uncommon Cents had taught me the difference between Common Cents that you spend and Uncommon Cents that you keep.

"Have fun, and say 'Hi' to Pine-e-wah and Ben. I've put some cookies in your backpack for them. Make sure they get some." She opened the front door.

I ran out of the house, still excited.

"Did you remember your cell phone?" Mama yelled.

"Yep!" I answered as I ran down the driveway.

"Be careful, and remember, five o'clock! Or else!"

The bus came right on the dot, eleven o'clock. One thing I could be sure of, the town's bus system was top notch. Geepa had always counted on it for his transportation, and he often set his watch by their schedule.

As I sat at the stop, I could see the bus's blinking yellow lights coming down the street. I realized the scar-faced driver—Earl—could be driving. I shuddered at the thought, but quickly decided I'd have to get over my fear of him in order to make trips on the bus alone. But as it came closer, I could see the driver was a new person that I'd never seen before.

I was sure the two dollar bills were Common Cents before dropping the first one in the bus's toll box; then, I took a seat in the back and watched the familiar scenes pass by, impatiently waiting for the stop at my destination. When at last it arrived, I jumped from the bus into a snow drift, working to pull my legs to the surface. "Be careful out there, kid," the driver said. "The snow's deep and there've been reports of wild-life wandering around." Then he closed the bus door and drove off.

I jogged, building momentum to slide on the icy tracks the cars had made on the road. Slip-sliding down the country road to Ben's house, I kept my eyes on the chimney to see if there were signs of a nice warm fire.

"This is going to be an awesome day, you guys!" I told my Uncommon Cents in the pouch.

"Yeah, well just remember the Rule we made, we get in on the action, too!" Two Bits reminded me from inside the pouch.

At last I could see smoke rolling out of the chimney at Ben and Pine-e-wah's house. I was relieved to know that there might be a nice warm hearth waiting for me there. I ran down the driveway and up to the kitchen porch. Pine-e-wah came running before I could knock on the door.

"Well, look who the North winds blew in, Ben!" he turned and yelled back into the house. Reaching out to me, he pulled me inside and hugged me. Ben came running into the kitchen and tackled me with such gusto that he laid me flat on the floor right in the middle of their kitchen.

"Hey, Oli!" he shouted. "Geeze, what took ya so long?"

"That's no way to greet a girl," Pine-e-wah said.

"Those are fightin' words to her," said Ben.

We both laughed as I got to my feet. After I took off my heavy coat, we settled in the living room, and I scooted up close to the fire. Taking the pouch from the pocket of my flannels, I carefully placed it on the table next to me, opening it only enough for my friends to listen. Pine-e-wah watched as I set the pouch down.

"Oliver told me he planned to give you the pouch someday," he said, looking at me. "I'm glad to see you're carrying it with you." He and Ben looked at each other and smiled.

"Yeah, Geepa wanted me to take care of it for him," I explained.

"Glad to hear that, kiddo," said Pine-e-wah, "it meant a lot to your Gramps. Probably the dearest treasure he owned." He and Ben smiled at each other again and shifted their chairs closer to the fire with me.

I went on, explaining Dad's ridiculous reason for not wanting me at Cardboard City and how Mama let me come out for the day, so I could check on the food supply. We talked about the latest news in town and at Cardboard City while we drank hot chocolate and ate bear salami and goat cheese and saltine crackers.

It wasn't long before Ben was ready to go. He stood and began taking cups and dishes into the kitchen. "So, Grandpa, I think we'll walk over to Cardboard City now," he said to Pine-e-wah.

"I was there last Monday, Ben. Gus is the only one keeping the fires warm. I don't know where all the others are this year," he said with a bit of concern.

"What do you think has happened to them?" I wondered.

"Don't know, kiddo. Maybe they figured since Oliver died, there'd be no more food, no reason to come out of the mountains."

"They'll die up there … won't they, Pine-e-wah?" I asked.

"You betcha, they will, too cold and too much snow. Why the wildlife can't hardly survive up there."

Faithfully, I unloaded the cookies and Geepa's picture from my backpack that Mama sent with me.

"That Abby, she's a fine lady," said Pine-e-wah. "Never will understand what she sees in your dad, but love is a crazy thing. Makes you lose all sense of reason." He quietly laughed and leaned back in his chair.

Pine-e-wah went on to reminisce about how he was once married. He and his wife had only one daughter whom they had raised on the reservation in Lapwai. When Ben was only five, both women were killed in a car accident. Ben's dad left him shortly after that. Pine-e-wah adopted Ben, and they moved north where they bought the farm. Life there required a great deal of work, so Pine-e-wah kept Ben home, so he could help with the chores part of the day and work on his school the rest of the day.

Ben said he liked being homeschooled; he loved hands-on learning. "Grandpa, I remember you once said there are things books can't teach," he said.

Ben must have learned a lot from books though because he could add numbers like no other. He was a reader, too; he knew every adventure story ever written. When we explored in the woods around Cardboard City, he would tell me how it reminded him of the last adventure story he'd read.

Resting back in his chair, Pine-e-wah suggested that we be careful what route we took to Cardboard City. "Walkin' the road is safest. Longer, but safe," he said. "Seen wolf tracks around the house lately. Haven't seen the animal with my own eyes, but it's wanderin' around here."

I then closed the pouch and returned it to the pocket of my flannels. Ben and I were ready for the trek.

Pine-e-wah had cows to feed in the barn, so he said he'd stay home. As we headed out the door, he stopped us and handed Ben one of the knives from the gun closet. "Keep this handy, Ben. Can't think you'll need it, but better to not need and have than to need and not have." He clipped the sheath to Ben's belt. "Take these with you, too," he said, reaching for two sauce pans on the drain board.

"What are these for, Grandpa?" Ben asked.

"Need some more pans at Cardboard City. Bring back the two worst of the old ones." He handed one to me and the other to Ben.

Ben took his pan and gave Pine-e-wah a curious look.

Ben and I headed out the door talking about the route of passage. Since time was short, we decided to take the ill-advised route over the hill, rather than

95

the long winding country road—in spite of what Pine-e-wah had told us. I could faintly hear the shouts of disapproval coming from my shirt pocket, but I ignored the protest. Ben called for his two dogs, Tina and Shorty, to join us.

By the time we reached the top of the hill, we had walked for nearly fifteen minutes and made good time. The wind had blown most of the snow from the hilltop, making for an easier trek. With Cardboard City now in our sights, we had only a thicket of trees to navigate, and then we could run down the other side.

As we hiked, Ben was telling me all about the new adventure book that he was reading. In this particular book, a plane had crashed in the mountains, landing in a small lake. The surviving boy was forced to make successive dives under water to search for survival equipment in the cockpit of the plane. There, he would have to maneuver around the corpse of the pilot who was still buckled in his seat.

As I pictured the ugly and sickening scene in my mind, I heard the snapping of branches in the bushes beside us.

Ben heard them, too, and we both froze.

"Move to the clearing," he ordered quietly.

I did as I was told, following Ben as he led our painfully slow exit from the bushes. As we went, we saw movement off to one side. Massive paws and yellowish-green, piercing eyes made my skin crawl. The wolf was huge, its mouth foaming with saliva, its teeth dripping greedily. My mouth wanted to form words, but I found it impossible. Even if I had decided what to say, there would be no voice to say it. For a fleeting moment, I considered screaming, but then realized that it would be ridiculous; a silent scream would be useless.

"Don't turn your back on him!" Ben whispered. I'd never seen Ben act so courageously. He took charge of the situation—but not quick enough—the wolf began to move toward us.

"He's after the dogs," Ben said quietly.

He grabbed the pan from my hand and started banging the pans together as hard as he could, hoping the noise would scare them off. Then everything became a blur. Ben was hollering and banging, the wolf was growling and rushing all around us. As quick as I would turn to face the animal, it would be behind me; Ben and I were nearly stumbling over each other trying to keep the wolf in front of us while protecting Shorty and Tina.

But the wolf was fearless.

Then I saw more of them creep out from the bushes into the open. Clearly, we were outnumbered.

"Take the pans! Start banging them!" Ben yelled.

Ben forced the pans into my hands and pulled the knife from its sheath and crouched, advancing on what I now realized was the pack leader, the alpha wolf.

Then there were gun shots.

We both fell to the ground, taking cover, and laying in fetal positions, utterly terrified. We were surrounded. Not knowing where the shots were coming from, we were afraid to move.

"Who's shooting?" Ben yelled at me.

Lying only a few feet away from him, I desperately tried to find my voice, but it failed me at every attempt. I simply lay on the ground, completely helpless. I had abandoned the pans and turned my attention to protecting Tina and Shorty.

The wolves didn't seem the least bit scared by the shooting. Instead they closed in on us more furiously. They were close enough for me to feel their growling snarls; their fangs snapping inches away.

Ben knew he had to do something, and between the two of us, he was the only one armed with a weapon, except for the mystery shooter. The surrounding mountains played games with the sounds of gun shots; the sharp crashes echoed back and forth. It was impossible to tell where the shooter was. I managed to reach out and grab Tina, and then Shorty, holding them closely to my chest. When the wolves saw the dogs tucked close to me, they began to focus the attack on me. I was without a voice. I had to find the courage to do something or, I, along with the dogs, would be torn to shreds. "Help me, Ben!" I screamed at last.

Rolling over to look in my direction, Ben could see what was happening. He rose to his feet and then yelled in awesome fury, throwing himself knife-first toward the alpha dog. Hearing a cry from the animal,

I knew Ben had made contact.

I lifted my face from where it had been buried in the snow and saw an old half-blind and crazy-looking man wielding a pistol, firing it randomly in the air.

It was Gus. He had heard the pans banging, the wolves snarling, and he had run up the hill shooting wildly.

Ben was bent in a battle stance with his knife still in hand. He and the injured wolf were circling each other, neither one retreating.

I quickly got to my feet; I held tightly to the dogs collars, knowing I had to do something to help. I turned toward Gus and yelled with all my might, "Gus, help us! It's Oli and Ben!"

The pack, affected by the injury to their leader, stopped their circling. I could see blood oozing from the hind quarters of the leader; he clearly favored the leg with the wound.

Ben and I continued shouting, "Gus! Help!" with everything in us, hoping Gus would finally recognize our voices and stop shooting.

The wolf pack retreated.

Then, running from the other side of the hill, we saw Pine-e-wah. His large body lumbered over the horizon, knife in hand, yelling Ben's name. The thought suddenly occurred to me that he knew full well we were likely to disobey and find trouble. He had sent the pans for reasons of signal, not kitchen use.

Ben was behind me backing away from the wolves, backing towards me. When we backed into each other we screamed in startled terror, and dropped to the ground. I turned on to my side to find Gus standing over me. Trembling, struggling to breathe, I tried to stand, but stumbled back to the ground and vomited.

Pine-e-wah moved toward the wolf pack, and they turned and ran. Satisfied, he then came to us, our frightened and limp bodies in a heap on the snow, Tina and Shorty lay beside us.

"Are you hurt?" he asked breathlessly.

"No. Just scared to death," Ben replied quietly.

Gus bent down beside me and stroked my hair. "Long time no see, kiddo," he whispered kindly.

Once Ben and I recovered, we all walked down the hill toward Cardboard City. Ben and I continued to tremble from fright even hours after the attack. We had not taken good advice, and we had paid the consequences. Even in his fear and anger, Pine-e-wah didn't lecture us. He knew the best scolding that we could have was the one we were giving ourselves.

Chapter 12

The Bus Dilemma

Our return trip from Cardboard City was by way of the road. The pans weren't really needed, as we suspected, so Ben and I carried them back. We walked behind Pine-e-wah with shoulders hunched, and heads hung low, Tina and Shorty faithfully by our sides. The pans we carried were like a ball and chain, reminding us of our bumbling mistake.

Once we arrived at Ben's house, Pine-e-wah insisted on walking me to the bus stop. Embarrassed and exhausted and cold, I asked him to let me make the short walk myself. He said that he would keep an eye on me until I safely caught the bus. Ben and I hugged—which was not something we had ever done before—but it seemed the right thing to do after surviving a near-death attack from wolves.

Going home would be unlike coming to Ben's. There would be no jubilant entrance into my house. Instead of lightly sliding my feet on the ice, I dragged them heavily. I would have to face the jury sitting inside the coin pouch sooner or later, but the prospect of more shame combined with the bitter cold was too much for my humiliated spirit.

As I neared the bus stop, I could see the bus's lights winding along the curvy country road. I reached into my coat pocket to retrieve the crisp dollar bill for my bus fare. To my horror, all I felt were chunks of snow. Anything I had stored in my pocket, including my cell phone, was now replaced with the remains of my terrifying episode on the hill.

In a panic, I began pulling snow and frozen dirt from my pocket. There was no money to be found. I quickly looked back, toward Pine-e-wah, toward Ben, toward their house so filled with warmth, but I realized they couldn't help with my dilemma. I had been so irresponsible. How would I explain myself to the new bus driver, especially after he had warned me of wild animals?

Then, even worse, the thought occurred to me: what if my pouch had also fallen from my shirt pocket during the calamity with the wolves? Pulling my soaking wet gloves off, I fumbled with the zipper of my coat and then reached desperately into my shirt pocket. I nearly cried with relief because my Uncommon Cents were safe. With all the panic, bare survival, and embarrassment, I had forgotten to check on them. I hated myself even more for that, for not being more careful with them. I took the pouch out, opened it, and winced.

There was little movement inside. No one was speaking. Their breathing was faint.

"Please. Tell me you're all safe and not hurt."

"Define 'not hurt,'" Penny said somberly.

"What's happened to you?" I pleaded desperately.

"We took a good crushing. Nanny's leg is hurt.

The rest of us are bruised and cut up a bit from my hair," Penny said.

"How bad is she?" I begged fearfully.

"She'll need medical attention—and quick."

"I've lost my bus fare for the trip home! Plus my cell phone … I don't know what to do." The tears started coming.

"How much do you need?" Buck said, standing bravely to his feet. The meaning of what he'd said wasn't lost on any of us.

"A dollar," I answered.

"I'm a dollar," he sadly conceded.

I got the feeling that he thought I would sacrifice Geepa's coin in order to get home. It sickened me. I stood in the dim light staring at them, speechless. I had never faced such a desperate decision. Spending Buck on bus fare would mean losing him forever. We were family, I realized. I knew Dad would see to it that I would never see Pine-e-wah and Ben again if he had to drive out to their house to get me because I had foolishly lost my bus fare.

None of my choices appealed to me. Every muscle in my body ached from the fright, and my head was still spinning in shock. At no time during the afternoon had I been able to think clearly. My Uncommon Cents were injured, none of us were in any condition to fix my money problem, and giving one of them up would be the worst betrayal that I'd ever committed. But betraying Geepa's trust would be even worse. My friends were few, too: losing Ben's friendship would mean spending every Saturday for the rest of my life locked away in my room.

I could see myself dropping my injured coin in the jail of the bus's metal toll box, never to see him again. What would happen to him? Who might take him? What kind of horrible treatment might he suffer? The conversations we'd had played through my mind as I remembered him, very frightened, telling me of wishing wells and casinos and laundromats.

I could hear the whining engine of the bus coming closer; I had to do something.

Nanny spoke then, in her broken, painful, and distressed voice: "Be honest."

"Yes, tell the driver what happened," Dimeon said.

"But what if he tells Mama and Dad about how I nearly died? They'll kill me!" I argued. I was sure the driver would leave me stranded. Either that or he would drive straight to my house, jump out of the bus, and tell every detail to my parents. My choices were grim but I was desperate. On top of all this, I was about to drop from utter fatigue. I had nothing left to trust in but my Uncommon Cents. They were right. They were always right. I should have listened to them four hours earlier.

Finally, the bus pulled up, and the door opened. With pouch in hand, frozen feet, and tearful eyes, I looked up at the driver.

The face of the man staring back at me frowned; his bright purple scar pulsed in the cold air. It was the dreaded Earl. "Well, kid, you gettin' on or just warmin' up the air out there?"

"I've lost my money."

"Well, what's that you got in your hand, kid? Looks like a money pouch to me," he said.

Before I could say anything, he looked closer, first at the pouch, then up at me.

"Get in the bus, kid. Let's get you home."

I was sure that he meant by that statement that he would escort me right to my door step, where he would unload not just me but the truth about my penniless state.

Clutching the pouch, I got on and walked cautiously to a seat as far away from him as possible. He waited for me to be seated, watching my every move. There was no one else on the bus. It was the end of the route. From times past, with Geepa, I knew that Earl would drive from here back to the beginning to start the route all over again.

I felt an eerie chill move through me. While never taking my eyes off the front of the bus, I opened the pouch and whispered quietly, "I'm scared."

"Don't worry, Oli, he's okay," said Penny.

"Just try talking to him," Nanny pleaded. "You'll see. He's a nice man."

Moments of silence passed as I built up the courage to speak. After a while, I cleared my throat and spoke, breaking the silence. "Thank you, sir. You have no idea how glad I am for this free ride. I promise I'll pay you back."

"Can't hear ya, kid," he yelled gruffly.

"Move closer," Buck said.

I moved from the rear seat halfway to the front of the bus and cautiously sat on the edge of one of the seats with my feet ready for my escape—if needed. "I said thank you for the ride. I promise to pay you back."

"No, ya won't. Your grampa would've done the same thing. I'm just doin' what I think he would've done."

Moving one seat at a time, I approached the front of the bus with a careful eye on Earl.

"That Grampa of yours was one of a kind," he continued. "I bet ya miss him."

"Yes, sir, I do. More than ever."

His sharp, cold voice changed then. For the first time, I saw his smile. As we talked, I slowly moved to the front of the bus and took a seat right behind his. The ride home was unlike any other bus trip that I'd taken with him. Earl's hard edges began to soften. I told him about the close call with the wolves, but asked him not to tell my dad—that is, if he knew my dad.

"Don't know him. But I do know this about him: he wouldn't be caught dead on public transportation."

I smirked and agreed.

As we approached my stop, I thanked Earl again for the free ride, and he thanked me for the good conversation. I stepped off the bus and turned to face him. "Please don't tell my mom about the wolves either."

He smiled and winked, "It's a deal, kid. My lips are sealed."

I turned and ran for the house, looking back to wave at Earl. The ride home changed my mind about the creepy bus driver with the purple scar. He was no longer the mean, gross driver I had feared; he was a life saver, a friend. I had wrongly judged him by his appearance.

But I had to get to my room quick. Nanny needed help.

"I'm home, Mama!"

"Good! Only ten minutes late, too. How was your

day?"

"Great! Everything's fine at Cardboard City." That wasn't a lie, either.

I ran upstairs, quietly shut the door to my room and pushed the lock.

I opened the clasp of the pouch and four wounded friends emerged. The fifth one sat in the pouch looking at me with wary eyes: Nanny. I carefully removed her and inspected her leg. I was no doctor, but I could see the cut was deep; I would have to find a way to close the wound.

The others watched as I performed surgery on a very brave lady. Although I knew that she was in great pain, I had no choice but to use the tiny needle and dental floss. Without stitches she could suffer from infection.

After I had cared for everyone's cuts, bruises, and bumps, I turned the shower to the hottest temperature that I could stand and stood under it, crying in long sobs. What kind of friend was I? Geepa had entrusted me with their care—and friendship. I had not only let them down, I had betrayed Geepa's trust.

Chapter 13

Aunt Gabby

*W*hen I returned to school the next week, Mr. Edwards, my sixth grade teacher, started a science unit entitled *Animals of the Wild in Northern America*. One entire week was devoted to wolves. Since the reintroduction of wolves to the mountains of Northern Idaho, the subject was a hot one in our class. We spent a lot of time arguing among ourselves. The kids whose parents were ranchers and farmers were angry about the wolves' presence, and the kids living in town thought they were beautiful animals that should be allowed to roam freely in the wilderness.

I had a different take on them—though no one would ever know. My Uncommon Cents and I had decided to keep quiet about our encounter with the wolves on the hill near Cardboard City. Word could spread, and if Mama found out, the results would spell disaster.

Mr. Edwards had assigned group projects that involved working with three other classmates of our choice. We were to make a physical migration map for whatever animal our group chose. Three of my friends and I, who were all children of farmers or ranchers, formed our group and selected our animal of choice: the wolf. Wyatt, Kaleb, and Parker all lived on the same side of the mountain as Cardboard City. We spent much of the next few weeks working together during class on our project. It was hard for me to remain quiet about my experience with Ben, Tina, and Shorty.

Friday before our project was due, the four of us were at my house working in the kitchen. Mama was helping us build the plaster on ply-board map of the mountains around our town. Her cell phone rang, and since we were all elbow-deep in plaster, she carefully set it on speakerphone. We could hear as the shaky voice on the other end started talking about her trip to the doctor. Quickly turning off the speaker, Mama clutched it desperately, covering it in green plaster.

"Oh no, Gabby! Tell me it isn't so," she cried in horror, tears filling her eyes.

I knew right away that this call was not good. She left the room crying and gasping between words while trying to talk. The four of us continued to work on the board, but I became increasingly worried. The boys sensed my discomfort and wondered if we should finish the project later. We worked quietly until the plaster for Paradise Ridge was finished. I was relieved when their parents finally arrived to pick them up.

The house was quiet; Mama had finished her phone conversation with Aunt Gabby. I went looking for her, and as I came to the top of the stairs, I could hear Mama and Dad talking, their voices coming from his office. I tiptoed quietly to the door and listened.

"I've got to go, Simon, this is urgent," she pleaded.

"What will I do with Olivia while you're away?" Dad said, in a panicked voice.

"It's not like she's the family pet, Simon, for crying in the night! She's your daughter."

"I didn't mean it like that, Abby. What I meant was that I have a job. And I'm very busy."

"Well, you may just have to act like a dad for a few weeks."

A few weeks, I thought. *This is trouble*. I ran to my room and closed the door behind me. It was disastrous. A few weeks alone with Dad were a death sentence.

I pulled the pouch from my pocket, opened it, and asked if they had heard the discussion between Mama and Dad.

"Only bits and pieces," answered Penny. "Fill us in."

"A few weeks alone with Dad! Mama's got to go somewhere, something to do with Aunt Gabby."

"Well now, that's a nasty kettle of fish, kid," said Buck. "No sense plannin' any fun. We'll be hanging out at that bank he runs pretty much twenty-four seven!"

"He's worried about what he'll do with me," I said sarcastically.

"This will present a problem for your father," added Dimeon.

"What do you mean, 'a problem for my father,'" I snapped back. "It's a *huge* problem for *us!*" I was hysterical.

"Easy does it, kid," said Two Bits.

"It's not going to be easy though! We've got to figure something out."

Penny was calm. "Maybe you can talk your Mama into letting you stay with Pine-e-wah and Ben…"

"No. She's insisting on making Dad be a dad while she's gone." I said, gazing out the window. The thought of escape briefly raced through my mind.

"Oh now, that's a real problem," said Dimeon, climbing from the pouch to rest on my hand. "As I see it, your dad will be faced with a responsibility with which he is completely uncomfortable. The situation will be very awkward for him," he reasoned.

"No kidding," I agreed, hoping someone would suggest a quick solution.

They had all come out of the pouch except for Nanny, who was still sore from her surgery. They formed a circle—which had become routine when problems occurred—and each thoughtfully looked in a different direction.

I was startled by a soft knock at the door.

"Oli, may I come in?" It was Mama; her voice quiet.

"Quick," I whispered, "back in the pouch, everyone!" There was a quick scurry of tiny feet while I laid the pouch on my hand, so they could easily file in.

"Sure, Mama. Come in." I made my way to the door. She stepped slowly into my room, looking around quizzically. "I thought I heard you talking to someone in here."

"Ah. I was just talking to myself," I stammered.

"Where are Wyatt, Kaleb, and Parker, did their parents come for them?" she asked.

"They went home." Looking at Mama with

concern, I asked, "what happened to Aunt Gabby?"

Her face was sad. "She has cancer, Oli," Mama announced.

"Will she die?" I asked worriedly.

Mama sighed. "Hopefully not." Her eyebrows wrinkled with worry. "She's going in for surgery on Monday. I'm leaving tomorrow, so I can be with her." Tears began to stream down her cheeks, and she sat on the edge of my bed.

I didn't know what to say to help her feel better. Aunt Gabby was a great lady, funny and lively. Then I thought of my cousins and wondered how they were handling the news. Aunt Gabby and Uncle Hal had three sons, two who were identical twins my age. Even though we didn't see each other more than once a year, we had fun together. The thought came to me: what if things were different? What would I do if Mama had cancer? It made me feel sick inside.

"So, Oli," she began, "you and your dad will be on your own for a couple of weeks."

I knew she could see the horror on my face.

I glanced up to see Dad standing in the open door, bracing his hands on the doorframe to support his tall body.

"Don't you worry about a thing, Abby," he said to Mama, "we'll be just fine on our own." His tone of self-assured authority disgusted me, it always did.

Mama turned to me. "Please mind your dad, Oli. And do as he says."

"Yeah, sure," I answered.

"Good. I'm going to start packing. My flight leaves first thing in the morning."

"Did those boys go home, Olivia?" Dad asked.

"They have names," I answered.

Mama slipped past Dad's body, still braced in the door, and walked briskly away down the hall to avoid the brewing argument. Once she was safely out of earshot, Dad stepped into my room and crossed his arms. His tall figure loomed over me, and he stared down, drilling me with his deep brown eyes.

"There's one thing you'd better get through your head right now: there will be no arguing and no talking back. I don't care if those boys have names—or for that matter, who they are." He turned toward the door to leave. "And they won't be coming over anymore until your mom returns home."

"Yes, sir," I answered sarcastically.

But he turned and disappeared down the staircase.

I stood motionless, feeling the anger, the rage running through me. If Geepa was still alive, I would have been sent to *his* house while Mama was gone. Now, from every perspective, I was doomed for disaster.

Chapter 14

The Face Off

*M*ama left for Aunt Gabby's early the next morning.

I missed her even before she left.

I was alone with Dad in a very inhospitable house. I tried to help myself to breakfast: I opened a package of Top Ramen and ate the noodles dry with a sprinkling of seasoning powder on top.

"What are doing, Olivia?" His voice sneaked up on me, making me jump.

"Eating breakfast," I replied coldly.

"Why don't you eat something healthy, like a bagel with cream cheese and a glass of milk?"

"No thanks." My interest in chatting with him was about as great as my interest in eating bagels and cream cheese, which I hated. I leaned against the sink and watched him make his morning cappuccino.

Chocolate milk *did* sound good on second thought, and I was thirsty from the dry noodles. We busied ourselves in silence, finishing our breakfasts.

"It's time to go," he said as he wiped the table clean.

"Where?"

"You're going to work with me today. It's about time you learn the business of finance."

"But it's Saturday," I protested.

"Money doesn't sleep, and it doesn't take vacations."

I laughed under my breath. He obviously didn't know my money.

When Mama was home, Saturday mornings were freebees. Once I cleaned my room, I could do as I pleased, which typically included texting Ben and making plans for the rest of the day.

Ben and I had a long standing agreement about Saturdays. He needed a change of scenery from the country, and I needed the same, but from the city. Whoever texted first on Saturday mornings earned the privilege of choosing the location.

If for some reason I couldn't spend the day with Ben, I retreated to my room, where I played checker tournaments with Nanny, Penny, and Dimeon. They would calculate the moves while Buck and Two Bits shoved the checkers from square to square. I had no problem beating Dimeon and Penny, but Nanny was unstoppable. When we became bored with checkers, I would put in Two Bits' favorite video game: *Secret Wars of the Swamp*. He would step wildly all over the control buttons, hurling himself around the controller like an expert.

This Saturday, however, would obviously be much different. After Dad insisted I change into pants without holes and a shirt that resembled something more like "what a girl would wear," which ended up as a button-up shirt with pockets, we left for a day of boredom and lectures.

Pulling out of the garage, he waited for the automatic garage door to completely close before leaving the driveway. Dad always locked the house down tight for fear that some "vagrant wanderer" would rob him blind. I thought he would be surprised if he only knew that all the "vagrant wanderers" in town wanted was a warm place to sleep and a hot meal—which they'd never get in our cold stone house.

I had taken my seat in the back, which, when I was alone with him, was my seat of choice. We drove through town, and I quietly talked with Penny about how Dad's life lacked imagination and laughter. If I didn't have anything to say about the Dow Jones Industrials, I was of no use to him or the conversation. "What is the Dow Jones, anyway?" I asked Penny.

Buck interrupted our conversation before it even got started, suggesting some great ideas for having fun that involved the escalators and trying to guess the bank's safe combination.

In no time, we arrived in the parking lot of First National Savings and Loan.

"Olivia, what are you doing back there?" Dad asked, turning the car off.

"Nothing," I answered.

"Look at me," he demanded.

I looked up at the back of his head and waited for him to turn around.

"Here, Olivia. Look up here."

I looked up to where he was pointing. Eyes staring at me in the rearview mirror, he studied me. "You've been talking to that coin pouch since we left home," he said, glaring.

"I'm just looking in my coin pouch." I stated indifferently.

"No, you're talking to it."

I sat motionless, staring back at him. Those eyes meant trouble. But there were no words. No excuse came to mind. I just stared back.

"I've seen you rubbing that pouch before. You look into it as if there's something alive in there. You remind me of Grandpa when you do that. You know he had a crazy obsession with that pouch."

"What's the matter with that?" I argued weakly.

"You're not going around town talking to a coin pouch! My reputation is very important, and it will not take a beating over your strange behavior. I've already been ridiculed by my colleagues about your grandpa's imaginary relationship with his ridiculous coin pouch. I'm telling you right now: it's going to stop. Whatever is in there is coming out." His eyes were fixed on mine through the rear view mirror.

I was scared, and then I became terrified. How would I hide my Uncommon Cents from Dad's greedy eyes?

"I'm going into the bank, and I want you and that pouch inside with me pronto. We're going to get to the bottom of this." He opened his door and began to get out.

"They're just coins, Dad!" I sounded more desperate than I wanted to sound.

He turned and ducked his head back into the car. "Well. They're probably worth something then. You bring them in, and we'll find out just what they're worth," he said cheerily.

"I'll never get rid of them, Dad; they were Geepa's coins, and I'm not selling them."

"Oli," he sighed, "you have a lot to learn about money. Besides, it's time for you to stop hanging onto the past. You have a bright future to look forward to."

It was obvious what he meant: that my "bright future" would be because of all of *his* hard work and money.

"I want you inside with that pouch and its coins, right now."

He stood, and I watched him button the jacket of his expensive suit and slam the door shut.

I heard the click of his shoes as he walked toward the glass double doors. How I longed to hear the musical sound of Geepa's shoes on gravel, walking beside me.

I sat in stunned silence. I looked through the windshield at the sign in front of the car: RESERVED FOR BANK PRESIDENT.

"I have a lot to learn about money, huh. But he doesn't know the first thing about money!" I stated angrily to my family in the pouch.

I was filled with anger and fear. I had to get my Uncommon Cents away from Dad, and he would surely already by now lecture me for taking my sweet time obeying him. Dad had told me to get inside "right now."

I looked at the clock above the car radio.

The thought occurred to me then that the bus would arrive at eight o'clock AM: I had five minutes to run four blocks and get them to safety.

Although I had no money for spending, I knew Earl was the regular Saturday driver. I could catch the bus to Pine-e-wah and Ben's house where I could safely hide my pouch from Dad.

"Let's go, guys. I'm getting you away from him. This may seem crazy, but I've got to get you all to safety. I only have five minutes." Having warned them, I was panting with fear and dread.

"But, Oli—" Penny was going to try to argue against my decision, but I knew time was wasting. I assured them that it was all for the best, snapping the clasp shut and securing the pouch in my shirt pocket.

I exploded from the car—not even shutting the car door—and ran like mad for Sixth Street.

I dodged by-standers who were converging on downtown for the Saturday open air market. With the bus stop in sight, I had only to cross one busy street and run half a block in order to reach safety.

Glancing quickly west, then straight into the bright morning sun to the east, I shot out into the street.

The city bus was too close to stop, moving too quickly. Still blinded by the sun, I heard the distinct sound of screeching tires, the smell of hot asphalt.

I saw one last thing: the horrified face of the bus driver and his bright purple scar.

Shattering glass resounded thickly through my head, a sound in slow motion. Pain shot through my back and legs. Sudden warmth covered my eyes, blurring my vision.

Then my world went black.

Chapter 15

Spinning Rooms

The days following were just the constant spinning of lights and the voices of people I didn't know. Sometimes they were quick and forceful. Other times the same voices would be low and droning. I couldn't tell if it was a dream or if the room was spinning and the voices were narrating the agony that my body was feeling.

I do know that I had one dream, though, because I had it again and again.

Geepa was in my bedroom; the door was closed. He sat at my bedside trying to wake me from a deep sleep. A tapping at my door would then wake me quickly, and I would spring from the bed and rush for the door, bracing against it, trying to keep it closed. The wooden door would then begin to swallow me, wrapping around me tightly. I would try to fight against it, but fell hopelessly through it toward the hard marble floor in the hall. Sharply pointed toothpicks, but huge, would then fill the hallway, pouring in on top of me, and I would suffocate from their weight. I would yell for Geepa, but my voice was gone. Then the room would spin up again and the foreign voices would drone in the background.

When I regained consciousness, Mama's voice was what my heart ran toward. I opened my eyes, but my body lay motionless. What little my vision registered was random machinery all around me, beeping and buzzing.

I made my first attempt to speak. The sound of my own voice was strange and rough, but it helped make everything more real, which was good. "Mama," I whispered.

She was gently rubbing my arm, but the pain of her hands on my skin penetrated all the way to my feet.

"That hurts," I pleaded with her.

"I'm sorry, honey," she was quietly crying.

"You're hurting me," I repeated.

"I'm so sorry! I was barely touching you," she said, in distress.

Nurses came from all directions, and there was a great deal of confusion for the next few minutes. I had to close my eyes because the quick movements of those around me made the room start spinning again.

"Tell them to stop moving," I begged.

"Honey, what do you mean?"

"The people moving are making me dizzy. I feel sick."

Mama told the nurses to move away from the bed, asking me to open my eyes again. I was relieved to see her face, her beautiful blue eyes.

"Where am I?"

Mama began to explain how I'd been hit by a city bus and was in the hospital. I had been unconscious for two weeks.

"Water. I'm thirsty."

She was careful to move slowly as she retrieved a cup filled with ice chips. The cold water from the ice on my tongue was the first good sensation that I'd felt.

I recognized the voice of our family physician, Dr. Boden. "She will need to go to a nursing home for some time, in order to recover and rehabilitate." I sensed the discussion wasn't one I was supposed to hear.

"No, she won't go to one of those horrible places." I cringed at the sound of Dad's whispering voice. "We'll pay for hospice to look after her in our home."

"No, Simon. We will not." Mama abruptly left my side to join their discussion, her voice sounded more authoritative than I'd ever heard it. "She *will* go to a nursing home. Oli will be good medicine for the people in the home, and they will be the same for her." Although the pain in my body was unbearable, the sound of Dad's voice brought tears to my eyes. I hoped Mama would return to my side so I could ask her to have Dad leave my room.

I'd been to all the nursing homes in town with Geepa and I knew even though the rooms were small and the halls smelled, it would be much better than the mansion dad insisted was home. Geepa had taught me how to talk to the old people. Mama was right; my stay there would be better than home.

"Abby, I think that's ridiculous," he said quietly, trying to persuade her differently.

"Isn't it time for you to go to work?" she snapped angrily. "Wasn't it you who said your money doesn't sleep or take a vacation? If so, it certainly doesn't take sick leave, either," sudden relief swept over my body.

There was no argument from him. Even though I couldn't see past my nose, I knew he'd taken his orders and left the room. Mama returned to my side.

"There have been a few changes at home, honey. When you're well enough to talk about them, I'll explain."

"I want to know now, Mama. What's happened?" Although I could now tell my condition was serious, I needed to know how our lives had been changed as a result of it.

"The renters have moved out of Grandpa's house. I'm living there alone for now." She went on to explain that she and Dad were having problems getting along. Their differences had grown too big to ignore. "We're getting professional counseling. We're committed to working through our problems, but for now I just need some space. I think you understand"

It was not just that her voice changed. It was that she finally *had* a voice; it was more reason for relief and comfort. My body lost sight of it's pain, and for a brief moment tears of relief washed my face.

It was this relief that allowed me to let go of things just enough to jog my memory. "My pouch! Where is it?" I was panicking.

"I don't know, Oli—calm down, honey. It wasn't on you when the paramedics arrived at the hospital." she looked concerned.

"He took it!"

"Who? Who took your pouch?"

My memory was very clear. I had been desperate

to get my Uncommon Cents to safety. "Dad. It was Dad I was running from," I cried softly. "I was running for the bus stop. I was going to get away from Dad," I explained.

"Why?" she asked quietly but insistently.

"He said I would have to cash in my coins; he was not going to put up with the same ridicule he'd had with Geepa," I blurted out angrily, "but no one can do that, Mama, they're *my* Cents." I winced at the pain in my head.

Slowly, at the corner of my eye, emerged the figure of a man: "Earl," I whispered.

Chapter 16

Earl

I don't know if it was the pain of my body or the pain of my soul, but the room began spinning again, and voices once again droned. Everything went dark.

The next time I awoke, Ben was sitting beside my bed. His was the face of a friend. I could hear Mama and Dad in the room mumbling back and forth with Dr. Boden.

"Hey," Ben smiled.

"Hey, how long have you been sitting there staring at me?"

"Long enough to be sick of seeing your eyelids. Anybody home in there?" Still, he was the same old Ben.

At the sound of my voice, Mama rushed to my side. "How do you feel, Oli?"

"Pretty good. My head feels like it's been squished, and I'm sore. Aside from that, pretty good."

Mama's smile looked forced. "Do you feel well enough to talk to your dad?"

I didn't think that I'd ever feel that well. I figured I'd have to face him sometime, so it might as well be sooner rather than later. "Sure," I answered grudgenly.

"I think it's time we get the story straight, Simon. I want the truth," Mama said sternly. "Is it true? Did you tell Oli you were going to take her coins and cash them in?" I could tell Mama was making an attempt at diplomacy, but her anger was peeking out through the cracks.

Dad didn't answer.

"Where is my pouch?" I asked, trying to sit up in bed. I pulled myself up far enough to see my legs locked in braces, suspended from pulleys over the bed. "My legs! What has happened to me? And my coins! Where is my pouch?" I screamed in panic.

"Shhh, lie back," Mama calmly insisted. "You've broken your legs and fractured your pelvis. And honey, you have a serious concussion."

"But my coins!" My panicky screaming was starting to hurt me.

Mama turned to Dad. "Where is the coin pouch, Simon?"

I heard him make quiet muttering sounds, and I tried to sit up again. "What did you do with them?"

Mama gently laid me back on the bed.

"I didn't touch the pouch." Dad finally answered, on the defensive.

"Where's my shirt? They're in my shirt pocket!" I yelled.

"Where is her shirt, Simon?" she questioned him bitterly.

He answered, "I had the medics put her bloody clothes in a plastic bag, but there was no coin pouch in her shirt."

Then from the corner of the room near the door, a familiar voice quietly spoke out: "When I was a boy, living in the loggin' camps, my old man made me run once, too."

Dad looked shocked. "Who are you?" He peered at the figure hiding in the shadows of the corner.

Earl ignored his question. He moved slowly toward my bed. "I was fifteen that summer. Henry, who was the loggin' camp cook, gave me a couple silver dollars for helping out in the kitchen. My old man was greedy, and he caught wind of the money and came after me with his huntin' knife. He was thinkin' he was gonna teach me a lesson about having somethin' he didn't." Earl's eyes locked onto my own, and he pointed: "He left this scar on my face to remind me there'd be *none* of that."

He then turned to face my dad. "Sounds kinda like that's what happened here."

Dad didn't say anything.

Earl continued, "Maybe what the kid's got here is somethin' bigger than money. Maybe, you're mad that she got somethin' you think you shoulda got."

"Those are bold words, and they're not true." Dad replied angrily.

"That fancy suit you wear, that big house on the hill, that deluxe car you drive ... they don't entitle you to nothin', mister." Tension filled the room. "Oli woulda never run out in front of me had you not chased her off. She feared for the only treasure she owned, and you were gonna just *take it from 'er.* You ain't deserve no more treasures, big shot ... 'cause you don't know how to take care of the ones you got."

"You've got a lot of nerve talking to me like that!"

Earl wasn't backing down, and he wasn't finished. He put his pointer finger right into Dad's chest. "The problem with you is that just 'cause you got money, you think people love you as much as you love yourself. My daddy put a scar on my face where everyone can see it. You put a scar on the kid's heart where ain't no one gonna see it but her. But don't make no difference where they are—a scar's a scar and they reminds ya of somethin' painful." Light and authority poured right out of Earl, and Mama, Dad, Ben and the nurses in the room stood breathless, watching and waiting for the next move.

"All that money you got's taught ya nothin' except how to get more. But that ain't what it's about, big shot. Real treasure ain't found on the stock market or in a bank. Treasure's in the folks we care about." The whole room was motionless—it remained that way.

Earl turned from Dad and bent over me. He smiled, winked, and said, "I'll be back, kid."

"Over my dead body," Dad spoke indignantly.

Earl looked back over his shoulder. "That'll work, too." He turned and left as softly and mysteriously as he had entered.

Silence gripped the room tightly. The nurses turned and left, leaving only the four of us.

"So it's true. Simon, isn't it," she demanded, as she moved from my bedside to face him at the end of the bed.

Dad looked away from her and moved to the door.

"Looks like our problems seem to be growing, don't they Simon?" Mama's anger had turned to quiet sobs.

Dad left. He didn't return for months, but that's another story.

Chapter 17

Sunshine

I woke early the next morning to the sound of clanging trays and squeaky wheels on the meal cart in the hallway. I felt pleasure for the first time as the smell of bacon wafted into my room. Bright pink rays of sunrise shone through the partially open blinds.

Earl quietly approached my bedside. "Good mornin', kiddo."

I was surprised to see a visitor so early in the morning. "Hey, Earl. It's early, isn't it?"

"Yep. I like watchin' the sunrise. Do it every day."

"Thanks, Earl. I mean for yesterday. You told my dad what I couldn't put into words."

"I got a little surprise for ya. Want it now, or should I come back?" He reached for his shirt pocket.

"What is it?"

It was the greatest surprise I could have received. The metal of the clasp caught the light and I knew immediately. "My Cents!"

"Yep. Case ya didn't know for sure, I was the first one at the scene of the accident." He smiled at me. "I knew what was goin' on that split second when I saw the look in your eyes as you ran out in front of my bus. Your old man was gonna take 'em, and you wasn't about to let him have 'em. If it wasn't for you coverin' your face and chest with your arms, your Cents would have been thrown helter-skelter."

He carefully placed the pouch on my chest opening the clasp. There were five of the most beautiful faces I'd ever seen. I wanted to hug, squeeze, and kiss every one of them, but I resorted instead to tears of joy and relief. "I didn't think I'd ever see you guys again!" I was blubbering like a baby.

"We knew we'd see you! That is, if you pulled through alive," Buck said, a quiver in his voice.

"I've got more reasons to live now than I did a minute ago," I laughed and cried at the same time.

"So, you knew about them, Earl?"

"Oh sure. I've known about them for a long time! Whatcha think your grandpa and I talked about on all those bus rides back and forth from Cardboard City?"

"Really?" I was so shocked I could have been pushed over with a feather. Maybe that wasn't quite true, since I was as pushed over as anyone could be.

"Don't worry, kid. Your secret's safe with me. And anytime ya need it, your coins are safe with me too."

I heard a soft knock at the door and reluctantly asked my Uncommon Cents to scurry into their pouch. The door opened wide enough to see another friendly face peek in. Pine-e-wah smiled, and entered the room. Earl reached out his hand to Pine-e-wah, and they firmly shook each other's hands, and then smiled and winked at one another.

"Looks like we'll have all of them around for a lot

longer, huh, Earl?" Pine-e-wah smiled from ear to ear looking at the coin pouch and then gently squeezing my big toe that was now black and blue from bruising, and sticking out from the end of my cast. Dimeon was the first of my Cents to peek out from the pouch,

"Well, howdy, little friend!" Pine-e-wah knelt on one knee looking Dimeon face to face.

"Bonjour, Monsieur Pine-e-wah, how wonderful to see you again." I suddenly realized there was a lot to my life that I didn't know about. Who knew my secret, or was it even a secret at all?

Epilogue

*M*y soul came back to life that day. It would take months in the nursing home before my legs would return to normal. I had to learn to read, write and walk again, and it took a longer time to regain the strength to climb Paradise Ridge.

My memory was also damaged, but not enough to recall what happened during my twelfth year—which, as it turned out, became one of the most meaningful years of my life.

I've come to see the whole accident as a gift. Mama and Dad finally had to face their problems, which, once it all came out, answered a lot of the questions that puzzled me about them. Dad and I would have some work ahead of us. We had a lot more to deal with than just water under the bridge. It was more like a raging sea under a tiny rowboat.

There was something about Earl looking out for me all those days in the hospital that changed me; I stopped feeling sorry for myself. If the people I valued the most believed I was worth a lot, then shouldn't I do the same? Dimeon called it an, "epiphany", I just think Geepa got the Fourth of July feeling up there, and gave me the blessing.

The accident and everything that led up to it taught me about the value of people—especially small coins with legs—and people with ugly scars.

The scar on Earl's face became a beauty mark to me. Every time I looked at it, I was reminded of his value as my life-saver and friend.

I was just like Earl, I realized. I had scars, too, but mine were on my legs. We both shared scars on the outside, but what really connected us were our scars inside.

I also learned a good lesson about money, about real worth. Earl and I agreed: some things in life have greater value than they're worth. For Earl, what was valuable was giving people safe bus rides worth a dollar. For me, what was valuable was caring for five small coins worth only a dollar forty-one.

My Uncommon Cents taught me two important lessons. It's often the most unlikely folks—like small coins with big hearts and bus drivers with gruff voices—that end up being those we trust most. And it's not losing the expensive things in life that breaks us. What bankrupts our soul is when we don't care for those small treasures that—in reality—have great value.

Perhaps only Earl and Pine-e-wah will ever believe that I own money that talks, but I don't care. Penny, Buck, Two Bits, Dimeon and Nanny are worth millions to me. Sure, their value as money is a dollar forty-one. But to me ... they're worth all the money in the U.S. Treasury.

I wonder how many other coins need good owners who will value them for all they're worth?

Oh, and one other lesson I've learned: money talks. We just have to learn to listen.

CPSIA information can be obtained at www.ICGtesting.com
Printed in the USA
BVOW012346170412

287943BV00004B/1/P